THE ADVENTURES OF
LAZARUS GRAY
VOLUME NINE
THE SINKING WORLD

BY BARRY REESE

PRO SE PRESS

REESE UNLIMITED

THE SOVEREIGN CITY PROJECT

Also available by Barry Reese from REESE UNLIMITED
and published by Pro Se Press:

The Peregrine Omnibus - Volumes 1-3
The Adventures of Lazarus Gray
The Adventures of Gravedigger

Other Works
The Family Grace: An Extraordinary History
Rabbit Heart
The Damned Thing
The Second Book of Babylon
Assistance Unlimited: The Silver Age – Broken Empire

THE ADVENTURES OF LAZARUS GRAY, VOLUME NINE: THE SUNKEN WORLD

A Reese Unlimited Book
Published by Pro Se Press

"Secrets of the Dead" Copyright © 2014, 2015, 2017, 2020 Barry Reese & George Sellas
"The Sunken World", Musings From The Author, and "Timeline" Copyright © 2020, Barry Reese

Cover Illustration by George Sellas
Print Production and Book Design by Sean E. Ali
E-Book Design by Antonio lo Iacono and Marzia Marina

New Pulp Seal created by Cari Reese

Edited by Mike Hintze
Editor in Chief, Pro Se Productions-Tommy Hancock
Publisher and Pro Se Productions, LLC-Chief Executive Officer-Fuller Bumpers

Pro Se Productions, LLC
133 1/2 Broad Street
Batesville, AR, 72501
870-834-4022

proseproductions@earthlink.net
www.prose-press.com

THE ADVENTURES OF

LAZARUS GRAY

VOLUME NINE
THE SINKING WORLD

THE ADVENTURES OF

LAZARUS GRAY

VOLUME NINE
THE SINKING WORLD

TABLE OF CONTENTS

SECRETS OF THE DEAD
THE ORIGIN OF LAZARUS GRAY
BY BARRY REESE AND GEORGE SELLAS

PAGE 1

෨෬

THE SINKING WORLD
AN ADVENTURE STARRING LAZARUS GRAY
AND ASSISTANCE UNLIMITED

PAGE 5

෨෬

MUSINGS FROM THE AUTHOR

PAGE 157

෨෬

THE REESE UNLIMITED
TIMELINE

PAGE 161

THE SOVEREIGN
CITY PROJECT ™

SECRETS OF THE DEAD
THE ORIGIN OF LAZARUS GRAY

LAZARUS GRAY

IN SECRETS OF THE DEAD

BY BARRY REESE &
GEORGE SELLAS

BORN TO WEALTHY SAN FRANCISCO PARENTS, RICHARD WINTHROP ATTENDED YALE UNIVERSITY AND GRADUATED WITH HONORS.

BUT ON THE DAY OF HIS GRADUATION, HE WAS APPROACHED BY WALTHER LUNT, WHO OFFERED HIM A PLACE WITHIN THE SHADOWY ORGANIZATION KNOWN AS **THE ILLUMINATI.**

HIS NATURAL INTEREST IN THE SUPERNATURAL SUDDENLY UNLEASHED, RICHARD ACCOMPANIED LUNT AROUND THE WORLD, INVESTIGATING THE UNKNOWN.

ALONG THE WAY, HE MET MIYA SHIMADA, A LOVELY JAPANESE-AMERICAN WHO WON HIS HEART.

BUT EVENTUALLY WINTHROP LEARNED THE TRUTH ABOUT THE ILLUMINATI AND THE VILE SECRETS THAT THEY POSSESSED. REBELLING, HE BECAME AN ENEMY TO THE MEN AND WOMEN HE HAD ONCE TRUSTED.

SHOT AND LEFT FOR DEAD ON THE SHORES OF SOVEREIGN CITY, RICHARD WINTHROP HAD NO MEMORY OF WHO OR WHAT HE WAS. THE ONLY CLUE TO HIS IDENTITY WAS A SMALL MEDALLION WITH THE WORDS 'LAZARUS GRAY' STAMPED UPON IT.

UNAWARE THAT LAZARUS GRAY HAD BEEN THE FALSE IDENTITY OF THE ILLUMINATI'S FOUNDER, WINTHROP TOOK THE NAME AS HIS OWN, IN THE HOPES THAT IT WOULD DRAW OUT THOSE WHO KNEW THE TRUTH ABOUT HIS PAST.

RESURRECTED AS A HERO, LAZARUS GRAY NOW FIGHTS TO MAKE UP FOR THE EVIL ACTS HE TOOK PART IN WITH THE ILLUMINATI. AIDED BY OTHERS WHO HAVE SIMILAR PASTS, LAZARUS GRAY HELPS MAKE SURE THAT THE INNOCENTS OF SOVEREIGN CITY CAN SLEEP PEACEFULLY IN THEIR BEDS!

THE SINKING WORLD

CHAPTER I
HAMMERFELL

February, 1941

COFFEE AND PAPERS flew into a mess as the two strangers collided on their hurried paths, unaware that their destinies were now intertwined.

"I'm so sorry," the pert young redhead declared, already stooping to try and gather up the papers that she'd dropped. Her name was Sally Weatherby and she was just twenty-five years old and newly arrived in Sovereign City. Having grown in a small Kansas town, she was still distracted by the hustle and bustle of life in the big city.

All around them, the throng of people separated, moving in two lines around them. It was like they were alone in a small pocket of humanity as men and women hurried to and from lunch.

"Oh, no, it was my fault. Completely." The gentleman that now wore a large coffee stain on his tie and white shirt quickly knelt and snatched up a folder that belonged to him before setting the remnants of his coffee in its cup on the ground so he could help the pretty girl with her own papers.

"I ruined your shirt," Sally said regretfully, pushing a lock of hair behind an ear. Her large green eyes locked on his for a moment and she felt a flush rise to her cheeks. The young man was rather handsome, and he couldn't be more than three or four years older than she. "I can pay to have it dry cleaned," she offered but broke off when the man waved aside her words.

"Nonsense! These things happen." He seemed to study her and for a moment she felt naked beneath his gaze. She was dressed quite fashionably, having spent pretty much every cent she had after renting an apartment on clothes for her new job. "If you really want to make it up to me, maybe I could take you to lunch one afternoon? You work in the secretarial pool at the Hawthorne Building?"

"Why, yes! How did you know?"

"I've seen you coming and going."

His admission that he'd noticed her before made Sally's heart flutter and she hugged her papers against her chest. "I'd like to have lunch with you... but I don't even know your name."

"John."

"I'm Sally."

"Nice to meet you, Sally." John looked at his watch and his good humor seemed to fade. "I better run. How about we bump into one another again tomorrow - same time and place?"

"I'll try not to make another mess of your shirt," she said with a shy smile.

John's reply was a quick grin and then he was off, losing himself in the sea of humanity that lined the city's busy city streets.

Sally stared after for a moment until several people bumped her with their shoulders. Without John there to make her part of a duo, she was simply an inconvenience, someone disrupting the natural flow of traffic.

As she started to turn and resume her trek down to a nearby office building, she looked down at the papers she held. They were mostly lines of business figures that Mr. Hawthorne wanted taken to his certified public accountant but to her surprise the top paper was not one of hers at all -- with a start, she realized that she must have picked up one that had slipped out of John's folder.

It was a drawing of an unusual looking item, one that it took her a moment to recognize. Sally realized that it was a Viking Age gold-plated silver pendant that was in the shape of an ancient hammer. Sally's father had been a mythology aficionado, so she was familiar with the stories of Mjolnir, the hammer of Thor.

Someone muttered something about her annoying out-of-towners and bumped their way past Sally. She started to protest that she lived her but she caught sight of a small object on the ground and plucked it up quickly -- it was the actual pendant, or one very much like it, that was depicted in the drawing. Holding it against her chest, she was surprised to find that it felt very warm to the touch.

She wondered what John did for a living... if he were here in this area every day, it was likely that whatever office he worked in was located in one of the many buildings that lined this city block. If she tried, she might be able to check the registry listings for each and try to figure out where he worked, then return the paper to him.

Of course, there was no guarantee that the drawing or the pendant was related to his work, which meant that she might not be able to figure out a connection between a business name and a hammer of Thor pendant. The drawing might have been a personal project or just something that someone else had given him -- and, besides, she already had plans to meet with him tomorrow.

Whistling softly to herself, she turned back in the direction of her task. The memory of John and his frank stare of appreciation stayed with her for the rest of the workday.

SALLY'S CAT, TIGGER, was waiting for her when she got home. Her apartment was small but comfortable and the rent was surprisingly affordable -- a side-effect of its location, she knew. It wasn't that the neighborhood was teeming with low-lifes... it was actually the opposite. She lived on Dent Street, which intersected Robeson Avenue... and everyone in Sovereign City, and quite a few places beyond, knew that 6196 Robeson Avenue was home to Lazarus Gray and his amazing Assistance Unlimited group.

The headquarters of Assistance Unlimited was part of a city block that was entirely owned by Lazarus Gray - which meant that Sally was actually a tenant in a building that he owned. What had once been an unassuming neighborhood had been transformed into the beating heart of Gray's law-abiding enterprise.

The centerpiece of his holdings was a three-story structure

that had once been a hotel. Gray's associates used the first floor, while the second had been gutted and converted into one large room that was used for meetings, briefings and research. The third floor was off-limits to everyone but Lazarus and his wife, serving as their private residence.

Facing the former hotel were several storefronts, all of which had closed down at the dawn of the Great Depression. They were now quite empty, though each was equipped with sensitive monitoring equipment that allowed Lazarus and his companions to keep track of every car or pedestrian that stepped foot onto Robeson Avenue. Sally had no idea if that equipment extended onto Dent Street but she sometimes fancied that one of Gray's assistants, perhaps the dapper Morgan Watts or even the young and somewhat exotic Eun Jiwon, was watching over her as she walked home at night.

Tigger hopped up on the kitchen counter, loudly reminding her that he had eaten all of his food earlier in the day. After setting down her purse, which contained both the drawing and the pendant that she'd picked up from John, she put a bit more in his bowl. She then gave him a few strokes accompanied by some baby talk before wandering into her bedroom to change out of her work clothes and into something more comfortable. She didn't expect any visitors so practically the first thing to come off was her brassiere, which led to a sigh of sudden pleasure. Men were so lucky - women's fashions were always pulling, twisting and compressing their bodies, while men's clothing was designed for comfort as well as appearance.

Sally took care of her toiletry before changing into a pair of comfortable pajamas. Mentally, she was trying to remember what programs would be on the radio tonight - she hoped that it would be a new episode of Inner Sanctum Mystery. The show had debuted only a few weeks ago - right after the start of the new year[1] and it had already won a legion of fans, including Sally. Every episode opened and closed with the eerie sound of a creaking door... and Raymond Edward Jones hosted the program in an appropriately sardonic way.

Almost on cue, she heard Tigger in the other room. He hissed twice just before Sally recognized the sound of her apartment

---

1 January 7, 1941 to be precise.

door rattling as the latch held firm. Someone was trying to enter her home...!

Trembling with fear, Sally wondered what to do -- if she screamed, she might frighten away whomever was out in the hall but she might also alert them to the fact that she was inside... and she'd heard enough horror stories about young women being raped in Sovereign to pause before doing that.

The phone was located in the front room, so she crept out there, spotting Tigger hiding under a table next to the couch. The door rattled again, and she saw the chain that held the door closed stretch taut. If they increased the pressure, they'd break in and then what would she do? She had no weapons aside from a couple of dull steak knives in her kitchen... and she was afraid that she'd be too frightened to even use those effectively.

A terrible odor reached her nose suddenly and she knew that it emanated from whomever was at her door. It smelled like something had died... or had spent a long time in a charnel house.

She picked up the telephone and tried to reach the operator -- there was nothing but a hissing silence on the line. Now even more frightened, she let the receiver fall from her hand -- it thudded on the carpet.

A voice came through the partially opened door - it sounded dry and raspy, as if the person speaking was in dire need of a drink of water. "The pendant... give it to me." Thin white fingers pressed through the crevice created by the door and the chain, wiggling in the air. She could see that the owner wore a white long-sleeved shirt and a black coat, both of which appeared to be quite dusty.

Sally's eyes searched for the pendant and she snatched it up from the interior of her purse, holding it tightly between her breasts. "Go away!" she said in a tremulous voice. "I've called the police and they're on their way!"

"You lie," came a hoarse reply, punctuated by a sharp bark-like laugh. The man on the other side of the door leaned more heavily against the barrier and the chain stretched even further. Sally saw it starting to give way and she knew that within seconds she would be face-to-face with her malodorous visitor.

Working on instinct, she lowered her shoulder and sprinted

forward. She grunted as she made impact with the door, but her action surprised the intruder and his arm was pinned as the door slammed shut on it. There was a horrible snapping sound as the arm broke and a grunt came from the other side, along with an exhalation of foul air.

Sally felt the figure on the other side thrashing against the door and she pressed her full weight against it. She was a tiny slip of a girl, though and it took all her effort not to be thrown away. The door did open enough for the man to pull his arm back to the other side, however, and Sally heard heavy footsteps as he thudded back down the hall.

Pressing her ear against the door, she listed as the man went down the stairs to the first floor, muttering all the while under his breath. His odor lingered and now that her adrenaline began to fade, Sally felt the urge to gag.

She felt something pulsing in her palm and for a moment she thought it was her pulse, hammering away... but it didn't match the pounding of her heart. Looking down, she opened her clenched fist and realized that it was the pendant, throbbing in her grip. Letting out a squawk of alarm, she tossed it to the floor... but in its absence she somehow felt both more frightened and weaker. She bent down to retrieve it, even as her cat slunk out from its hiding place and sought her out for comfort. With one hand she moved the pendant between her fingers while the other stroked Tigger's fur. Her mind was filled with questions... about John, about the stranger at her door and about the pendant.

When she had calmed down enough to try the phone again, she found that it was working perfectly. Despite this, she didn't ask the operator to summon the police. Instead, she put the receiver back down onto its cradle and sat down heavily on the couch. She set the pendant aside, planning to slip a length of cord through the opening at the top -- she'd wear it to work tomorrow in anticipation of giving it back to John.

Despite her weariness, she was wide awake. What if the intruder came back again? Somehow, she felt certain that he was done with her for the night -- but that thought wasn't enough to overrule the dread that filled her heart.

She and Tigger barely slept a wink.

⟨∞⟩

SALLY SAT DOWN in her chair at work, stifling a yawn. She had applied a little extra makeup this morning, hoping to hide the bags under her eyes but she knew that she wasn't looking her best. Still, it couldn't be helped.

She had picked up the newspapers on her way in, knowing that her boss frequently liked to read them when he made his way into the office. A quick glance at the itinerary for the day told her that there were no major meetings scheduled so she was hopeful that she could have a nice, quiet morning before she found John for lunch.

Unfortunately, her hopes were dashed as her eyes happened to fall upon the bold boldface that lined the newspaper headline: MAN CHOKED TO DEATH IN HOME, POLICE BAFFLED

Some feminine intuition brought a chill to Sally's blood as she lifted up the paper, unfolding it so she could read the article in full. It was all written out there in lurid detail -- a man by the name of John Watkins, aged 27, was found strangled to death in his home. The apartment appeared to have been ransacked and the force used on Watkins' throat was so strong that his windpipe had been completely crushed.

Sally felt warm tears come to her eyes and she tried unsuccessfully to blink them away. It was all so clear to her now: the same awful man that had come to her home had gone to John's, as well. Perhaps John had been forced to tell him that he didn't have the pendant and that he assumed that Sally might have picked it up... that's the only way she could fathom that the killer would have known who she was. But John hadn't learned her last name...! Perhaps it wasn't so obvious, after all.

The pendant seemed to grow warmer - it was hanging between her breasts, suspended on a leather cord. She clutched at it through her blouse and a decision was suddenly reached. Last night on her way home she'd been comforted by the thought of her neighbors, Assistance Unlimited. Perhaps they knew of the strange events that had transpired? If not, she owed it to John to alert them.

She stood up, grabbed her purse and headed towards the elevator. She passed her boss on the way, ignoring his murmured greeting. When the elevator attendant saw her, he recognized the look of a woman on a mission and he dispensed with his usual small talk. They rode in silence to the first floor and Sally was in motion before the door was fully open.

She hailed a cab and breathlessly whispered the following words to the driver: "Take me straight to 6196 Robeson Avenue!"

CHAPTER II
THE MIDGETS OF DOOM

LAZARUS GRAY WIPED at his temple with the back of a hand, smearing blood across his face. The cut was leaking at an alarming rate, but he wasn't worried - head wounds had a tendency to bleed profusely.

"Where is he?" a high-pitched male voice said.

"Hiding somewhere, no doubt. Like a mouse. Squeak! Squeak!"

The question and its slightly insane response came from The Bludger Twins, a pair of midgets that were wanted in three states for committing violent murders using hammers. Their real names were Tom and Terrance Sullivan and their sordid life stories were enough to turn the stomach of even the most hardened of crime fighters.

Raised by an alcoholic father and a prostitute mother, the boys had been incorporated by both parents into their respective vices... with their father, they sometimes raided liquor establishments and they quickly developed an addiction to booze. Their mother, meanwhile, sold them to men whose tastes ran to both the male and young. It was at the age of nine that one of them committed their first murder -- the twins had argued about it ever since, each claiming to be the one that had taken a hammer to one of their mother's johns. Regardless, they had learned that they never again had to feel helpless.

Lazarus hunkered down a bit more, hiding behind a stack of crates. This abandoned warehouse had become the brothers' hideaway and the leader of Assistance Unlimited had trailed them here after they'd brutally slain one of the city's few honest cops. Despite the efforts of Inspector Cord and Mayor Quinn, graft still had deep roots in the city and that was part of the reason why Sovereign had become home to so many vigilantes over the years - besides Assistance Unlimited, the city was the stomping grounds for Doc Daye, Fortune McCall and the ultra-violent Gravedigger, among others.

One of the twins - Lazarus wasn't sure which one it was -- rounded the corner and came into view. The diminutive killer was wearing a suit obviously designed for a child and in his right hand was a bloodstained wooden mallet. The man's face was a chilling mockery of humanity - his nose was bulbous; his lips were stretched taut in a sneer and his eyes were sunken into his skull.

"Here, piggy, piggy," the dwarf muttered, his pink tongue darting out to swipe across his lips as he completed the phrase. The little man hadn't spotted Lazarus, who was hidden not only by the protective cover of the crates but also by the shadows produced by the yellow glow of a light overhead.

If Lazarus had still held his gun, he would have fired it now -- it was the perfect shot. Unfortunately, one of the twins had caught him unawares - the hammer blow had failed to connect perfectly but it had been enough to cause him to drop his weapon.

He'd have to go back and retrieve the gun before the day was over. The powerful handgun – a .357 Smith & Wesson Magnum - had been introduced in 1934 as the most powerful cartridge pistol of its time. Capable of projecting a 158-grain bullet at about 1400 feet per second, the gun packed a major punch. Lazarus had taken an additional step by having each of the silver-tipped bullets soaked in holy water and blessed by a Sovereign City priest.

Tensing, the leader of Assistance Unlimited waited until the dwarf was within reach. Then he launched himself out of his hiding place, his shoulders slamming hard into the little man. The duo rolled across the floor, but the Bludger Twin held on tight to his weapon, refusing to lose his deathlike grip on it.

The miniature killer rolled a little distance away from Lazarus and was on his knees in a flash. The mallet whistled through the air and the hero was forced to throw his arm up to protect his head. The blow rattled his limb and sent pain rocketing from his arm to his brain. He wasn't sure that his left arm was going to be of much use for the rest of the battle.

Before the Bludger Twin could strike again, Lazarus struck out with his right hand. It was an open palm blow, catching the dwarf under the chin and snapping the man's head back. Lazarus closed his fingers into a fist and planned to finish off his foe when something small but heavy jumped onto his back. It was the other Twin, using the handle of his mallet to choke Lazarus.

"Look at his face turning blue!" the murderous man hissed in the ear of his foe. His cheek was pressed. "Look, my brother!"

The twin that Lazarus had struck was now scrambling to his feet, a drop of blood dripping from one nostril. He grinned in lusty pleasure at the sight of Lazarus struggling to breath. The hero's injured left arm was useless, so he was trying to push away the mallet with just one limb… and despite his greater size and strength, he was not in a position to free himself.

"Let me bash his skull in," the bleeding twin muttered. He hefted his mallet and Lazarus knew that he was in immediate danger of losing his life.

Before the fatal blow could fall, Lazarus threw his weight back, momentarily knocking the dwarf off-balance. He then forced his body forward, the mallet's handle digging painfully into his throat. Twisting his body, he was able to toss one brother over his shoulder. The twins slammed against each other and fell to the ground, allowing a gasping Lazarus Gray to struggle his way back to his feet.

The terrible twosome came at him with snarls and curses, each swinging their mallets with murderous intention. Lazarus tried to use his size to his advantage - he kicked out with one leg, striking one of the twins before he got too close. His shoe crunched down on the little man's nose, breaking it.

The second twin struck Lazarus three times in the side, badly bruising his ribs. Lazarus grunted with each blow and responded by driving his right elbow against the dwarf's skull. Before the killer could raise the mallet again, Lazarus seized him by his unwashed hair and yanked him towards the wall behind him. He slammed the man's head against it twice and then tossed his unconscious body aside.

The remaining twin spat out blood that he'd swallowed

and looked with fury at his fallen sibling. "You shouldn't have hurt him. He's the weaker of us. I always look after him. When he gets hurt like that... it makes me really, really angry." To punctuate his words, the remaining Bludger placed both hands on his hammer's handle and took a few practice swings through the air.

Lazarus was no longer willing to let either of the twins be the aggressor. His left arm and his ribs were both aching, and his head wound was still bleeding, partially obscuring his vision as some of the red liquid seeped into his eye. If he kept going like this, he was going to make a fatal mistake -- he had to turn the tables. Perhaps now that he was facing only one foe, he could afford to take more of a chance.

First, he moved one of his legs, positioning the toe of his shoe under the fallen brother's mallet. He kicked the weapon up into the air and snatched it with his good hand -- then he pounced, swinging the heavy mallet in a deadly arc that the other Bludger was barely able to block.

The two of them began trading blows, each being successfully parried by the other. The midget had the advantage of using such a weapon for many years, but Lazarus was bigger, stronger and quite skilled in fencing, three elements that he brought to bear against his opponent. It took nearly a full minute for one of Gray's attacks to get past the smaller man's defenses but when it did, the strike connected with the Bludger's chain and shattered the little man's jaw.

The midget fell to his side, dropping his weapon cradling his chin in his hands. Blood was streaming out of his mouth, soaking the floor. He muttered something but the words were incomprehensible. His eyes were wide as he looked up at Lazarus and his fear was almost palpable: he was afraid that the larger man would do what he would have done in this same situation. There was no killing blow to come, however -- Lazarus was made of different stuff than that. He tossed aside the mallet and reached into one of his pockets, pulling out a pair of handcuffs that he quickly placed onto the tiny fellow's wrists. He repeated the process with the other Bludger sibling and then stepped back, finally allowing his injured body a moment of respite.

Lazarus left the two men where they were as he went to

retrieve his .357. Once he'd holstered the weapon, he walked out to his car and used the radio to call the local police.

He was leaning against the driver's side door, unwrapping a stick of gum, when he heard the crackle of the radio. The police were slow to arrive, which was par for the course, so he opened the door and slid behind the wheel before picking up the microphone and depressing the button that allowed him to speak. "Yes?"

Samantha Grace's silky-smooth voice answered right away. "Are you on your way back? We have a client."

Lazarus heard the whine of sirens in the distance. "Give me about fifteen minutes to wrap up here and then I'll head that way."

"The lady's young and attractive so Morgan's keeping her occupied."

"I'll do my best to rescue her from that situation."

Samantha laughed in response. "See you soon, chief."

Lazarus looked over as a squad car came to a stop beside his own vehicle. Inspector Cord, whippet-thin as always, jumped out of the passenger seat and headed into the warehouse without sparing a backwards glance at Lazarus. Cord had recently broken up with Samantha and ever since he'd been a bit distant to the entire Assistance Unlimited team.

With a sigh, Lazarus exited his car. He ached all over and would be sure to toss a few aspirin into his mouth once he got back home. The Bludger Twins might have been small, but their mayhem level was large enough to leave an indelible impression on Gray's memory.

CHAPTER III
THE THUNDER WEAPON

SALLY'S EYES WIDENED as Lazarus entered the room where she'd been seated for the past half hour. She knew this building was a converted hotel and she assumed that this had once been a room reserved for business meetings... the way it was laid out made her think it had always been used for purposes like this.

It had been amazing enough to meet Morgan, Samantha, Abby and the even-cuter-in-person Eun... and she'd even gotten over her initial fear of The Black Terror... but seeing the famous Lazarus Gray was almost too much for the starstruck girl. With her heart hammering in her chest, Sally managed to stammer a word of greeting when the handsome leader of Assistance Unlimited said hello.

Gray was tall and possessed of a kind of lean physique that made her think he probably had no body fat at all. He was all hard muscle. His face looked like he'd been carved from marble and the dimple in his chin kept drawing her attention away from the tight set of his lips. The most interesting feature, however, was his eyes -- Heterochromia was what the condition was called, she remembered. One eye was a sparkling emerald in color while the other was a dull, ruddy brown.

Gray appeared to have been in a fight recently. His left arm was in a sling and there was a bandage over a wound on his temple. His clothing was immaculate, however, so she assumed he must have changed before seeing her. He wore a crisp white shirt, tailored slacks and a harness that contained a holstered gun on the left side of his chest.

For his part, Lazarus was taking in Sally's appearance in a quick glance. Young and eager, the woman was slender of build and the owner of a somewhat wide mouth that was quite attractive when she smiled. She dressed modestly and he had the feeling that this was perhaps her favorite blouse and skirt combination as it showed signs of frequent wear.

Samantha, seated to Sally's right, made the introductions. The pretty blonde was frequently taken for granted by the team's enemies as she looked like lovely but useless socialite... the truth was, she was an excellent fighter and able to speak seven different languages. "Sally believes that she might have information that could help solve the murder of John Watkins."

Lazarus nodded, having read the morning paper before leaving in pursuit of the twins. "Start at the very beginning, Miss Weatherby. How did you know Mr. Watkins?"

Sally recited the story with few flourishes but precise detail. Her boss detested frivolous notes inserted into the reports that Sally would type up for him, so she had learned to focus on the key details in the time that she'd been his secretary.

She completed her story by reaching into her blouse and pulling out the pendant. When Lazarus extended a hand, she pulled the leather thong over her head and allowed him to take the tiny hammer-shaped object.

"Morgan," Lazarus said after holding the pendant up to the light. "Can you please go and fetch my wife?"

The team's senior member rose and exited the room, his expensive shoes making hardly any sound at all on the plush carpet.

Sally's familiarity with Assistance Unlimited meant that she was well aware that Lazarus was married to Kelly Emerson Gray, the curator of the Sovereign Museum of Natural History. The statuesque redhead entered the meeting room a few moments later with Morgan in tow. Sally was impressed -- Kelly looked like an amazon in both height and beauty. She was a perfect match for Lazarus.

"Morgan said you needed me?"

Lazarus gave a nod and held up the pendant, letting it dangle from his fingers. "Does this look familiar to you?"

Kelly let out an audible gasp and she quickly snatched away the carved image of a hammer. "I'll be damned," she said. "It's even warm to the touch, just like the stories say."

Sally leaned forward. "Excuse me? Could someone tell me what's going on?"

Kelly glanced over at Sally, seemingly noticing her for the first time. Lazarus whispered something to her, and Kelly offered a smile and took a seat near the young woman. "At the museum, we recently acquired a strange metal box... we haven't been able to cut it open and the only thing resembling a lock we found requires a key that's in this shape. The man that sold us the box said that it contained one of the wonders of the world and that the key was formed of the same metal as the box and whatever object lay within. He also said that he was in the process of tracking down the key and would bring it to us when he had a chance... unfortunately, he was murdered before he could do so."

This time, it was Sally's turn to gasp. "John?"

"Yes. I'm sorry -- were you and he close?"

Sally shook her head. "We only met once. I'm afraid I ended up what that pendant quite by accident."

"John was what we call a reclamation expert. He traveled all over the world, locating artifacts that he could sell to museums and private collectors. My father and I have done business with him for a few years but there was something about this latest find of his that had him on edge. I think he was afraid that he was in danger -- and that's not all that unusual in his line of work. A lot of people are in the hunt for these things and sometimes he had to cross the line of what was legal to find them. I'll be honest and say that we didn't ask too many questions." Kelly looked over at Lazarus, expecting to see a look of disapproval but her husband was too lost in thought to let his feelings show.

"Am I still in danger?" Sally asked.

Eun answered her question. The young Korean-American adjusted the hat he wore and said, "The way I see it, you're likely to get another visitor unless we let it get out that you don't have the pendant anymore."

"Can you please do that? I don't think my heart can stand another evening like the last one."

"There may be other options," Lazarus said, preventing Eun from responding. "If need be, we might allow this person to come after you again so we could be lying in wait." Lazarus ignored the look of alarm on Sally's face and continued, "But first, we should try to use this pendant to unlock the box at the museum. It could be that once we have the item in our full possession that the killer might leave on his own."

"I don't really like the sound of that first thing you mentioned."

"I'd personally make sure that you were in no danger."

"Even so…"

Samantha reached out and gave Sally's hand a pat. "How about you spend the afternoon here and let us take the pendant to the museum? Hopefully, we'll never have to worry about using you as bait." She flashed her blue eyes at Lazarus, silently telling him not to push too hard on that point. The last thing they wanted was to drive Sally away -- if they did that, she would be on her own against whatever threats lay outside their headquarters.

Lazarus picked up on the signal and said nothing as Samantha answered, "Well, okay… but I do need to be home by this evening. My cat has to be fed. And my boss probably thinks I've gone insane or quit…!"

Morgan gave a chuckle. "Don't worry your pretty head about that. I called him a few minutes ago and told him you were with us. He seemed pretty concerned about you, but I don't think he's angry."

"Oh, good. Thank you," Sally said with a sigh of relief.

All eyes turned toward Lazarus, waiting for him to assign someone to guard duty for Sally. None of them wanted that task - not even Morgan, who was still eyeing Sally with appreciation. They were men and women of action, each of them subsisting as much off excitement and danger as they did food and water.

When he finally spoke, however, there was no complaint. Assistance Unlimited was like a well-oiled machine and they trusted Lazarus to know how to best deploy the various parts of their organization. "Bob, I'd like you and Abby to stay here with Miss Weatherby. The rest of you will accompany Kelly and I to the museum."

The team split into two groups, murmuring words of encouragement to each other. The Black Terror and Abby Cross stayed where they were and the fact that Lazarus left what were arguably their two most powerful members behind made it clear to all that he was concerned that Sally might still be in grave danger. Meanwhile, Lazarus exited with his wife, as well as Samantha, Morgan and Eun.

Sally closed her eyes. What a morning...!

THE SOVEREIGN MUSEUM of Natural History was a sprawling structure, standing in the heart of downtown. Comprised of twelve interconnected buildings, the Museum housed well over a million specimens, only a relative few of which were on active display. With a scientific staff of over a hundred, the Museum funded nearly four-dozen scientific expeditions each year, sending explorers out all over the globe. The Museum was divided up into numerous displays but the most popular was the ever-present Start of Sovereign Hall, where the origins of the city were examined. To access this, visitors had to stride through the huge entranceway, where they could stare up at a full-size model of a Blue Whale, which hung from the ceiling. The whale had suffered a good bit of damage a few years back, when Lazarus had sparred with an assassin, but it had been fully restored and was once again back in place.[2]

Kelly led the group through the museum's wide halls, smiling now and then at her employees and museum patrons. Many of these stopped in place and stared at Lazarus and his companions -- even those that lived in Sovereign were starstruck when the famous heroes were in their midst.

"Here we are," Kelly said as she closed the door behind them. She'd brought them to a small room that was used by the staff to analyze newly arrived artifacts. Resting atop a large table was a peculiar metal crate with an indention on the lid that was in the same shape as the pendant that Kelly held in her hand.

Morgan leaned forward to get a better look at the box. "How old is this thing?"

"We think it dates back to at least the 13th century, but it could be much older."

Morgan whistled and straightened back up. "What do you think is inside?"

---

2 Back in the second volume of Lazarus Gray!

"Could be anything," Kelly replied. "But whatever it is, it's important enough for people to kill over it." She held up the small carved hammer and took a moment to slip it free of the leather thong. After dropping the cord into her pocket, she carefully placed the pendant into the depression the top of the box. It locked into place with a click and she jumped back when the pendant began to twist, slowly rotating into a position where the "head" of the hammer was pointed upwards.

"That was unexpected," Samantha murmured. "Primitive gear mechanism?" she asked, looking at Lazarus.

The taciturn hero didn't answer, instead watching as the box suddenly opened on all sides. The four corners separated, each pulling back from the center and then contorting themselves until they lay flat on the surface of the table.

"Not so primitive," Eun said. All of them approached the object that was now exposed within the container -- it resembled a hammer but was rather small... in fact, Lazarus was certain that he could have hidden it in within his coat. It was made out of some sort of unusual metal, just as the pendant and box had been. The item was beautiful, looking nothing like the mallets wielded by the Bludger Twins... this was a work of art.

"Mjölnir," Lazarus whispered, a note of amazement in his voice.

"Meow-rear?" Eun asked in confusion.

"Mjölnir," Lazarus repeated, emphasizing each syllable. "According to Norse mythology, it's the hammer of Thor. Supposedly it's one of the most fearsome and powerful weapons in history, capable of leveling mountains."

"It's... smaller... than I would have pictured it," Eun said.

Kelly smiled. "Men are always obsessed with how big things are. According to Snorri's Edda, Mjölnir was forged by the dwarven brothers Sindri and Brokkr as part of a bet they had with Loki. The bet was that the brothers couldn't create a weapon as beautiful as Odin's spear or Freyr's foldable boat so Loki tried to sabotage their efforts -- it resulted in the handle being too short but otherwise the weapon was flawless."

Eun gave a shrug and elbowed Morgan. "Can't say I'm impressed. If Thor was so tough, why would he carry around a *hammer* as a weapon? I mean, is he a handyman or a warrior?"

Lazarus began speaking and with each passing word, Eun saw Kelly's eyes widen in admiration: *"Thus he gave the hammer to Thor, and said that Thor might smite as hard as he desired, whatsoever might be before him, and the hammer would not fail; and if he threw it at anything, it would never miss, and never fly so far as not to return to his hand."*

"Uh… what was all that?" Eun asked.

"He was quoting from The Prose Edda," Kelly said. "And doing a damned fine job of it."

Samantha hid her smirk, sensing how much her friend was impressed by her husband. If Lazarus and Kelly had been alone, Samantha had no doubt that Kelly would have given him a kiss on the cheek, if not more. "So, we have a hammer here… you don't really think it's the hammer of Thor, though… do you?"

"Certainly would explain why people would want to murder for it," Morgan said.

"Someone should pick it up," Eun said. "That's the best way to figure out if it's something magical."

"I vote for Lazarus," Morgan said. "He's our leader and he's got the most experience dealing with supernatural objects. If it does something weird like try to take over his mind, he's the best hope we've got for fighting it off."

"Well, there's Abby," Samantha pointed out. "Maybe we should wait until our resident witch is around?" She looked towards Lazarus and added, "But it's your decision, as always."

Lazarus took a step closer to the hammer and he thought he could feel a shift in the air pressure as he neared it. Whatever this object was - whether or not it was truly Mjölnir - it was no normal hammer. He was about to say that perhaps it would be safer to place a call back to headquarters and ask Abigail to come join them… but he didn't get to voice such a thought. Instead, the lights in the museum suddenly went out, plunging the windowless room into total darkness.

"What the hell?" Morgan asked. His hand automatically went to the pistol he wore in a holster under his coat. He unholstered the weapon and moved towards the door. He yanked it open and confirmed that the blackout wasn't confined to just their room.

Kelly said, "The emergency generator should come on in a

second."

"I don't think it will," Lazarus replied. "This is no accident."

"How do you know?"

"Call it a hunch." Lazarus joined Morgan in drawing his handgun and he nodded at Samantha and Eun to also produce their weapons. Samantha reached under her skirt and pulled out a small pocket pistol that she always kept strapped to her thigh. Eun slid on a pair of brass knuckles - he preferred to be up close and personal when it came to delivering pain.

Several screams from deeper in the museum - in the direction of the front entrance -- caused everyone to tense up.

Lazarus gave a quick nod to Kelly and Morgan. "Stay here and watch over the hammer. Samantha and Eun, come with me."

───—

The trio entered the foyer and found chaos under the great blue whale.

Seven men were the source of the confusion and Lazarus thought that their appearance marked them as very unusual, to say the least. Six of them were squat and rather hairy, with long reddish-blonde beards. These men wore furs and leather, with heavy cloaks slung over their shoulders. Each brandished either a battle axe or a short sword and the bleeding bodies of innocent men and women were strewn about on the floor, showing that these violent half dozen were willing to use their instruments of death.

The seventh man hung back a bit. He wore a dusty black suit and a white shirt. One of his arms was in a sling, which immediately made Lazarus think that this figure was the man that had visited Sally the night before.

Samantha and Eun shared a glance and a smile. Each of them had made the same conclusion as Lazarus had in terms of deciding which of their foes was the leader. As such, they had already divvied up the remaining six, each intending to take on three of the burly men. That left the man in the suit for Lazarus.

Eun launched himself at the nearest of the men, connecting with a roundhouse kick that knocked out one of the hairy man's teeth. Upon landing, the Korean-American immediately struck another of the men twice, punching him hard in the nose with the brass knuckles he wore.

Eun's third foe swung a battle axe at his head and Eun gasped as the blade caught his hat and sent it flying. A few inches lower and Eun's skull would have been split open.

The warrior with the newly christened gap in his teeth stabbed with his short sword and Eun was so busy dodging the battle axe that he was nearly skewered. The edge of the sword was dragged across his hip, sending a flare of red-hot agony to his brain.

Eun grabbed the swordsman's forearm and gave it a yank. The sword sank into the belly of the man with the missing tooth. Eun took advantage of the fellow's confusion and drove an elbow into his face. He then shoved the swordsman away, spinning around to face his remaining foe -- the man whose nose was streaming blood.

Dancing back a few steps, Eun winced as his injured hip flared with pain. He knew that the wound was slowing him down, but he considered himself lucky to be facing three brutes whose forte was pure violence and not skilled fighting.

The warrior bellowed an obvious insult at Eun, despite the fact that whatever language he was speaking was not one that Eun was familiar with. As the man came towards him, Eun kicked him in the shin and then finished him off with a brass knuckles punch to the side of the head.

Samantha was handling her own trio of foes with greater ease. While the men were armed with bladed weapons, she had her pistol -- and that allowed her to take them out without engaging them in melee. The first of the stocky men went down with a well-placed bullet between his eyes while the second and third attempted to avoid her shots but were felled as she emptied the clip into their bodies. She then turned to see if Eun needed any backup but by that time he was dispatching the last of his own opponents.

When both Eun and Samantha were left standing over the fallen bodies of their enemies, they exchanged breathless smiles. Samantha reached under her skirt to holster her empty gun, adding, "You look like hell."

Eun winced and touched his bleeding hip. He muttered an

obscenity under his breath, but Samantha merely laughed. She was about to reply when she noticed that both Lazarus and the man in the dusty black suit were missing.

"Uh oh," she murmured."

WHEN LAZARUS HAD first approached the strange man in the filthy suit, he'd noticed an awful odor emanating from the fellow, as well as his sunken cheeks and ghastly pallor. If not for the fact that the dusty man was walking about and blinking, Lazarus could have easily mistaken him for a dead man.

Both men had one bandaged arm and Lazarus was grateful that Morgan wasn't here -- the former Mafia man would have been incapable of not making a joke about the odd coincidence.

"You're after the hammer," Lazarus said, ignoring the sounds of violence behind him. He trusted Eun and Samantha to handle their side of things.

The man nodded. "Yes. Will you give it to me, or do we have to kill you?"

"Give me your name."

"Why?"

"Because I like to know who I'm fighting."

"Durok," the man answered. "And you are Lazarus Gray... a name associated with resurrection. Do you have such a power? If I were to slay you, would you return?"

"It's been known to happen."

"We'll have to test it again, I see." Durok too one step back and raised his good arm. He drew a circle in the air and suddenly Lazarus found himself outside of the museum, in a grassy field located to the east of the parking lot.

Durok was standing a few feet away, a grim smile on his face. "Do you see, Mr. Gray? You are out of your depth."

"Says the man that got his arm broken by a secretary and her cat last night."

A look of fury passed over Durok's face and he made the mistake of taking several quick steps toward Lazarus. He drew back his arm for a backhanded blow, but it never got the chance to land -- Lazarus lowered his uninjured shoulder and rammed himself forward. His full weight struck Durok in the midsection and knocked the man over onto his back.

Lazarus sat down hard atop the other man, using his knees to pin Durok's shoulders to the ground. He punched him in the face with his fist, noticing how the indention made in the man's skin seemed to stay in place for far too long - it was like the usual plasticity of a human face was completely lacking in Durok.

"You can't kill me," Durok said with disdain. "I am not like you... I was carved out of mud and earth, infused with the spirits of men that died in acts of debauchery. My master would merely create another shade just like me if you were to destroy this shell."

"And who is your master?" Lazarus asked, reaching down to seize hold of the man's collar. He twisted the cloth, applying enough pressure to Durok's throat that the inhuman creature had trouble breathing. Despite his protestations that he wasn't human, he seemed to feel pain and he had the same weaknesses that all men had -- he needed to breath, for one.

Gasping, Durok managed to push out the words, "He goes by many names and you would know only a few. He is the air, impossible to grasp but capable of great destruction when he is angered."

Lazarus leaned in close, ignoring the awful stench that wafted from Durok's mouth. "Why does he want the hammer?"

"He wants it so it can be destroyed," Durok said, his dead eyes suddenly lighting up with an inner flame. "You didn't expect that, did you? He doesn't want to use Mjölnir. He merely wants to ensure that no one can."

Lazarus released his grip on Durok and backed away with great haste. Something was starting to happen to the mystery man -- his body was suddenly losing its corporeal nature. Durok was transforming into smoke and Lazarus saw fear in the man's eyes, despite his claims to seeming immortality. "What's happening to you?" Lazarus asked.

"My master is displeased with me. He thinks I am weak. It is time for another me to rise, one that will have greater strength and the wisdom of my failures."

"Name your master!" Lazarus shouted.

Durok laughed, delighted to see that his enemy was angered by his lack of information. "I have given you a clue, mortal man! It is not my fault if you cannot grasp it!"

Lazarus fell silent as Durok's body drifted away on the wind, nothing more than ash and pinpricks of light. The man's dusty suit was left behind for a moment, crumpling to the ground as empty as Durok's soul had been.

"He is the air," Lazarus whispered, his eyes narrowing. His mind, a steel trap full of every small tidbit of information that he'd ever come across, was quickly running through all the possibilities. He finally came to one conclusion, one borne out by the hammer he suspected to be Mjölnir. In various poems from the *Poetic Edda*, there was a figure sometimes dubbed Loptr, which was generally considered to be derived from the Old Norse word lopt, which loosely translated meant air.

That figure was Loki, the trickster god of the Norse pantheon... half-brother to Thor... and one of the key figures in their legends of the end of days, the final twilight of the gods known as Ragnarök.

CHAPTER IV
BALDR

ABIGAIL CROSS WAS a witch, born and raised in Louisiana. While the temptation to go down the path of Black Magic had been strong, she'd resisted it, instead choosing to use her powers to right the wrongs of the world. This had led her to meet Assistance Unlimited during a battle with Jack-In-Irons[3] and eventually to join them. Since then, she'd come and gone a few times due to personal events, but she was happy to be a trusted part of the team again and her duties included overseeing Lazarus Gray's personal prison that housed their more unusual foes. Dubbed Tartarus, it was hidden away in the Sovereign countryside and was home to the likes of Mr. Death, various members of Murder Unlimited and The Torch.

Abby was a curvaceous beauty, with long black hair and a penchant for cleavage-baring attire. Because she knew that men desired her and was flirtatious by nature, this sometimes led to problems with other women. Indeed, she and Samantha had not been particularly close in the beginning... but over time, they had bonded, finding that they had more in common than they'd first assumed.

Even so, Abby realized her limitations. Sally had already looked her over with a slight hint of disdain so she didn't think the young girl would want to be a comforted by her at this time.

Unfortunately, the only other option was Bob Benton, aka The Black Terror -- and the odds of him being any better at soothing Sally's frayed nerves were next to none.

Bob Benton was a taciturn warrior, a pseudo-human grown in a plantlike pod by the government to become a super-agent known as The Black Terror. Garbed in a uniform adorned by

---

3 In the second volume of Lazarus Gray!

skull and crossbones on the chest, he had been meant to strike fear into the hearts of America's enemies. He had done so but only after breaking free of the government's control and finding a home with Assistance Unlimited. In recent years, he had veered to the edge of becoming too violent for Lazarus Gray's liking, but he had stepped away from the brink and had been visibly trying to temper his anger issues.

Abby wished that Eidolon had been able to do the same. Jakob Sporrenberg had quit Assistance Unlimited, claiming that the group was coddling criminals when they should have been killing them. Abby missed him terribly, but she'd always known that their romance was unlikely to last.

Sally stood up, smoothing the lines of her dress. "Is there a ladies' room nearby...?" she asked Abby, her eyes drifting down to Abby's decolletage and quickly moving back up to the brunette's face.

"Right down the hall, on the left. Just give a holler if you need anything."

As soon as Sally was out of the room, The Black Terror let out a sigh of annoyance. "Do you think you could handle this babysitting job without me? I have some things in the lab that I'd like to work on."

"And I'd like to be back at Tartarus handling some paperwork of my own. Lazarus asked us to watch over her and that's what we're going to do."

The Black Terror adjusted the scabbard that he wore along his left leg. He'd started carrying the cutlass a little over a year ago, which Abby thought was a very peculiar thing for a man with his superhuman strength to do. It wasn't like a sword could do any more damage than his fist could. "Fine," he muttered, though Abby knew that he meant anything but.

She was about to suggest that they take Sally into another room upon her return. Lazarus had purchased one of those new fangled television sets and even though there wasn't a whole of choice in terms of what to watch, just about anything was more interesting than staring at these four walls. A mechanized chiming sound cut off her words and brought a look of relief to The Black Terror's face.

"I'll check on it," he said, taking several strides towards the door before Abby could stop him.

———— ◦◦◦ ————

BOB BENTON KNEW the chiming signified that someone had set off one of the many alarms that lined the city block surrounding 6196 Robeson Avenue. These alarms were nothing unusual -- sometimes they accompanied the arrival of a tourist or reporter, often intent on snapping a picture of the team's famed headquarters. But on occasion they signified something quite different... a client, a delivery van or even an enemy.

The Black Terror entered a small room lined with monitors, each showing a high definition image of part of the city block. Lazarus had been at the 1936 Berlin Radio Exhibition where a demonstration was given of 375 line television with interlaced scanning. He had immediately decided to not only get such technology at his home but to improve upon it.

He spotted the man that had activated the alarm on the monitor showing the front entrance to the building in which he now stood. The figure was dressed in a blue suit, white shirt and dark blue tie. He was quite handsome with curly blond hair and features that spoke of sensitivity and kindness. He appeared to be well-built and tall, but he was leaning forward with one hand clutching his side under his coat. Bob had seen enough injuries to recognize one -- this fellow was badly hurt. As if in confirmation, Bob spotted something drip down from under the man's coat... it was blood.

Hurrying out of the room, Bob opened the front door. The stranger smiled in greeting just before his eyes rolled up into his skull and toppled forward. The Black Terror caught him and was surprised by how heavy the man felt. He gently lowered the bleeding man to the ground and pushed back the coat, revealing a deep wound in his side. It was gushing blood with every breath that the man took.

Bob reached his arms under the man and lifted him up, grunting with the effort. Normally he was capable of lifting a tank over his head... so he had certainly never had trouble hefting up a single human being - until now.

He backed into the foyer and shouted for Abby. He carried

the man into a room that served as the team's infirmary. Doctor Hancock had been the team's on-call physician for years, but he was still recovering from wounds he'd received several months ago[4]. As a result, Bob -- a chemist by trade -- had become their de facto staff doctor.

Bob shouted again for Abby, having set the man down on a bed. He ripped open the fellow's shirt, revealing a well-muscled body that was lined with scars, some of which appeared to be quite old. "Who the hell are you?" Bob whispered, his eyes growing wide.

The man murmured something in reply and Bob couldn't quite make out what he said. When the stranger repeated it a second time, however, he made out the words. It was his name, one straight out of mythology: "I am Baldr, he of the shining light of bravery."

❈

SALLY WAS JUST exiting the ladies' room when she saw the buxom woman named Abby came sprinting past. The running motion sent the dark-haired female's curves to bouncing and Sally was reminded of her own slim frame. She'd always been jealous of girls like Abby, which she knew to be silly -- but she couldn't help it.

"What's wrong?" she shouted at the other woman's back.

Abby spun on her heels, rushed back to grip Sally by the wrist, and then began tugging the younger girl along after her. "I don't know -- the alarm went off and Bob went to check on it. Then he started yelling my name."

Sally tried to pull away. "Shouldn't I stay behind then? What if it's dangerous?"

"Lazarus wanted you to stay with us, remember? You're safer with me than on your own."

Sally knew that was probably true, but she wasn't an adventurous person by nature and the idea of rushing towards danger went against her common sense. Still, she relented and allowed herself to be yanked towards the medical center.

They found The Black Terror tending to a shirtless man

---

4 As seen in volume 8.

with a terrible wound in his side. Sally blanched -- she'd never seen anyone in such a condition, and she hoped she wouldn't embarrass herself by vomiting. She turned away from the scene, staring at a copy of Doctor Hancock's medical degree that was framed on the wall.

"Who is he?" Abby asked, stepping up beside Bob.

"He said his name is Baldr."

"As in the Norse god?"

"Yes… take a look at what I fished out of his side." Bob held up a sprig of greenery.

"Is that… mistletoe?" Abby asked.

"It is."

"If I recall my mythology, that's the only thing that harm him… assuming this is the real Baldr."

"Even if it's not, he believes he is." Bob looked at her with a grave expression. His gloves were covered in splashes of red. "He's going to die, Abby. He won't survive being transported to a hospital and by the time Hancock got here, he'll have bled out. You're his only hope."

Abby nodded, looking towards the injured man. Since joining Assistance Unlimited, she'd made a serious study out of healing spells… it seemed like one or more members of the team were always in danger of dying. There were limits to what she could do, though, and she was afraid that Baldr's injury might be too grave. "I'll do my best," she said, laying her hands on the man's chest and belly. He was in great shape and she hoped that his obvious health would make this a bit easier.

She whispered a few words, ancient ones full of power… and she felt a transference begin to take place. She was calling upon the ambient energy surrounding her, allowing it to pass through her body and into Baldr's. His wound glowed softly, the tissues repairing some of the ragged damage done to them. The bleeding ceased but the injury refused to disappear completely. Even as Abby continued her spell, she sensed some sort of resistance… this was no ordinary wound - there had been potent magic involved in this.

Sally risked a glance over her shoulder and what she saw caused her to gasp aloud. Abby's hands were aglow with some strange form of light and she could see the stranger's wound looking better by the second -- though it still looked quite terrible. The brunette's face was contorted in obvious pain and a bead of sweat appeared along her hairline and then slowly rolled down her cheek.

With a shudder, Abby pulled her hands away from Baldr. She fell into Bob's arms and he supported her for a moment as she groaned, and her eyelids fluttered.

"Are you going to be okay?" The Black Terror asked.

"I'll be fine," Abby said. She moved away from her friend and took a few deep breaths. "I can't save him, Bob. Whoever attacked him has power that I simply can't match... all I've done is give him a little bit longer."

"And that, fair maiden, is gift enow."

Abby looked down to see that Baldr's eyes were open and he was struggling to lift his head. "Stop!" Abby exclaimed. "You have to take it easy."

"There is no time, I fear... as you yourself have stated. I have come here to issue grim tidings and my entry into Valhalla depends upon my completion of said task."

The Black Terror helped Baldr sit up and the handsome man looked pained as he swung his legs over the edge of the bed, letting them dangle to the floor.

"The hammer has been found... and its power may be the only thing that can save Midgard from the destruction that has come down upon us."

"The hammer?" Bob asked. He looked over at Sally, thinking of her hammer-shaped pendant.

"Aye. Odin has perished in battle with Fenrir, who in turn was slain by Víðarr. Thor has been murdered in a manner most foul and Asgard is no more. Now the rage of the gods comes upon the home of mortal men and women. Midgard shall sink beneath the cosmic waves even as the stars vanish, steam rises, and flames touch the heavens."

"Ragnarok," Abby whispered.

"Your wisdom matches your beauty," Baldr replied. He began coughing then and his wound began to bleed once more.

"But these events aren't right... Loki was bound by his own entrails after murdering you. He didn't break free until Ragnarok began -- at which point you should have been dead for quite some time."

"History is a cycle, replayed again and again," Baldr said. "But no two cycles are exactly the same -- there are differences and there is always hope. It was Odin's desire that the cycle be broken, and the world of mortal be free of its ties to our realm. Let us pass into legend and let the time of Man be true."

The Black Terror frowned, still supporting Baldr. "So, you're here to tell us how we can save the world?"

"That is my hope. I was dispatched by the All-Father just before he died. Loki has gone mad, worse than ever before. In terrible battle, he did gravely wound me but I, in turn, destroyed his fleshy shell. He drifts as a spirit on your world, still able to control his minions but unable to open a portal large enough to let in his allies most horrible. He will try to merge with a suitable mortal so that he might better carry out his dark tasks." Baldr suddenly retched and from his lips came a silvery fluid that glistened in the light. This was his soul, Abby knew... he had only moments to live.

"What do we do?" Abby asked.

"Use the hammer. Give it to one most worthy. Beware Loki and his minions. They will need power to open the rift. If they succeed in bringing Surtur and the others to Midgard, all is lost!"

Baldr abruptly threw his head back and more of the silver liquid exploded outward from his mouth and nostrils. He began convulsing and both Abby and Bob began shouting, trying to do whatever they could to keep him from hurting himself.

Sally slipped from the room, her heart hammering in her chest. She'd come to Sovereign with wide eyes and a hopeful heart... but the past two days had shaken her to the core.

She suddenly wished she were back home, curled up in the bedroom she'd had at her parents' house. Closing her eyes tightly, she tried to calm her breathing and regain some measure of self-control.

"It's going to be okay."

Sally opened her eyes to see that Abby had followed her. "That man... is he--?"

"Yes, he's dead... but the things he told us will help. We're not going to let anyone hurt you. You have my word."

"You must think me an awful fool," Sally said, blinking away tears.

"Why would you say that?"

"Because I'm out here weeping, feeling sorry for myself... and you're all calm and composed! I don't know how you do it."

"It's not easy," Abby admitted. "Some things you just get used to -- and you're not used to this, so it's perfectly normal to feel confused about it all."

Sally smiled in relief. "Thank you, Ms. Cross."

"Abby."

"All right... Abby."

The two women embraced briefly and then separated as Bob exited the medical room. He looked from one to the other before saying, "I'm still wondering what role John Watkins played in all this. Where did he get that pendant from? It seems unlikely that he'd just happen to find it when all hell is breaking loose in Asgard. There's got to be more to all this than coincidence."

"What do you have in mind?" Abby asked.

"As soon as Lazarus and the others get here, I want to pay a visit to John's apartment." The Black Terror made a fist. "One way or the other, I plan to get to the bottom of this!"

CHAPTER V
TRICKSTER

HE WAS, BY all accounts, an unremarkable man.

Mike Simms was of average height, not quite tall enough or short enough to warrant being put into either category. He was not fat, but he was possessed of a sort of pudgy softness that kept him from being accurately described as fit. His eyes were a forgettable shade of brown, not quite lovely enough to warrant attention. His facial features were a trifle too wide but nothing that caused any one to take a second glance at him.

He worked in an office on Eisner Avenue, toiling away as an insurance adjuster for Danny Colt Life and Health. He turned in his work on time but never went the extra mile that would have led to bigger assignments, Christmas bonuses or an office with a window view.

Day after day, he got up, brushed his teeth, got dressed, went to work and then came back home. He rarely read books, listened to the radio sparingly and had no major hobbies to speak of. His dating record was not much better, consisting of awkward dinners with the daughters or nieces of his mother's friends.

Mike simply *existed*, never really living.

———

STEPPING INTO HIS apartment around 6:45 in the evening, Mike reached out to turn on the lights. The first attempt caused the room to briefly illuminate before the light flickered back out. Sighing, he flipped the switch down and then back up, repeating the action twice before the light bulbs remained in a functional state. He'd spoken to the landlord about the shaky wiring in his apartment many times but he was always blown off - 'I'll look at it on Monday,' the man would say... but that particular Monday never seemed to come.

Tossing his coat and his briefcase onto the couch, Mike wandered into the kitchen and pulled a beer from the fridge. He twisted off the cap and downed half the beverage in one long swig. He belched and wiped his mouth with the back of his hand, setting the rest of the beer down on the counter.

He had some leftover Chinese in the fridge, but it was almost three days old and he knew it was time to toss it in the trash. If he did that, it would probably mean another night of peanut butter and jelly... assuming he still had any bread.

A strange sound caught Mike's attention. It came from the living room and sounded almost like footsteps... which was impossible, of course. Mike lived alone, with not even a fish to call company.

Still, thoughts of that murder he'd read about in the paper caused him to retrieve a steak knife from a nearby drawer. He brandished it in front of him as he moved to investigate, feeling a bit silly as he did so.

In the living room he spotted a man dressed in a dusty black suit. The man's color was sickly, and his skin was thin and leathery, with sunken eye sockets. The man's hands were buried deeply in the pockets of his coat and his lips were spread in a garish parody of a smile.

"Mr. Simms," the stranger purred. "I am Durok."

"What are you doing in my home? Get out!" Mike jabbed at the air with his knife, but the effect was far from threatening. He was obviously not an experienced fighter.

"I know that your life to this point has been... less than satisfactory. I am here to give you the opportunity to make a change."

"What are you talking about?" Mike asked but his resolve was weakening. Despite the strangeness of the situation, Durok had hit upon something very truthful: Mike was uneasy about the state of his existence. "Do you have some sort of job offer?"

Durok's awful smile stretched painfully wide. "I do indeed have an offer... you will be able to leave behind your failures and your disappointments. You will be important... powerful and wise. Men and women will bow down before you."

Mike stared at the stranger, taking in his ghoulish appearance... but still trusting him for some reason. Durok was telling the truth.

"I'm listening," Mike whispered.

───❧───

"**D**ON'T MIND THEM, they're dead."

Mike balked at the sight of the corpses and the awful stench of decay that wafted off of them. Durok had led him out of his apartment and into a dimly lit neighborhood before finally opening a manhole cover and inviting Mike down into the sewer system.

"I'm starting to think that I shouldn't be here," Mike admitted.

They were in a small room sealed off from the rest of the world by a heavy door that was marked CITY PERSONNEL ONLY. The dead bodies were all male and were dressed in sanitation uniforms... most of them looked like they'd been Caucasian but one or two were Negroes. It was hard to tell because they were all bloated and their skin had turned varying shades of white, green and grey.

"Nonsense," Durok replied, nudging one of the bodies out of his way with a foot. Mike hadn't known the previous version of Durok -- if he had, he might have wondered at the change in the man's personality. It was becoming slightly more deranged by the minute. Each version of Durok was slightly different from the rest, altered a bit by the chemistry of muck and grime that was used to house his immortal Asgardian spirit. "This is where you're going to be reborn, Mike. It may look like a lair of squalor and death but it's where you're going to become a god."

"Yeah, you've said something like that before. How, exactly, is this going to work?"

"Have you ever heard of Loki?"

Mike frowned. In school, he'd been a straight C student, always doing just well enough to get by but never really mastering the material. "I think so," he muttered without much enthusiasm. "He was one of those gods like Hercules and Zeus, right?"

"Not quite," Durok said. He had a strange look on his

unpleasant face and it took Mike a moment to realize that it was an expression of doubt... he wasn't certain that Mike was truly right for this 'gift,' whatever it really was. "Loki is a powerful god, the son of all-father Odin. In turn, he is the father to the wolf Fenrir, to the dangerous but lovely Hel and to the world serpent Jörmungandr. He is sometimes brave, sometimes cowardly but always scheming. He is my lord and master. And soon, you shall provide your mortal form to him."

"He's going to take over my body?"

"His own form has been destroyed. He needs a means of interacting with the mortal world -- and for some reason, he has decreed that you shall be the vessel for his spirit. You will still exist, and you will be aware of all that transpires but you will not be in total control. Loki shall direct your flesh. This is a tremendous honor."

Mike hesitated before gesturing to the dead bodies around them. "Who were these people? Why did you kill them?"

"Parts of their bodies were needed to revive me. If death dismays you, you will get over that. Loki's plan for this world will mean that it must be remade."

"People will die?"

"Many."

Mike pondered this and was a little bit surprised to find that it didn't trouble him. He hated the smell and sight of these corpses, but he hadn't known them, and he felt no empathy for their families or friends. "I'm willing to go along with that," he said at last.

"I knew you would be," Durok replied. He reached out and touched Mike's shoulder with a long-fingered hand. "Now comes the time when you will become the avatar for Loki."

"I'm ready," Mike said, though he wasn't quite as certain as he hoped he sounded. He wasn't a coward, but he wasn't brave, either.

Intense pain came with no warning, starting in Mike's gut and spreading out in all directions from there. He cried out and would have fallen to the floor had Durok's grip on his shoulder not held him upright.

Mike felt like his guts were being pulled from his body and he even looked down to make sure that wasn't the case... he saw now visible wound, despite the amazing agony that he felt. Just when he thought he couldn't handle any more, the pain was replaced by a new sensation, one that in some ways was equally disturbing -- he felt a second presence, a psychic one, entering his body. It took root in his brain and he felt his own consciousness being shunted aside. His body no longer felt like his own and it was as if he were looking through the eyes of a stranger.

Panic set in and Mike wanted to scream but his mouth was no longer his own. He wanted to flail his arms and tell Durok that he had changed his mind, but his body would not respond.

Durok stared into the face that had once belonged to Mike and he saw a transformation come upon it. He released his hold on the man's shoulder, allowing him to stand freely. Gone was the perpetual sense of hesitation, replaced by a firm purpose of will. This was no longer a mediocre example of a man -- this was Loki, the trickster god and he had wrought physical changes, as well as mental. 'Mike's' hair had been lengthened and was now reddish in color -- and the lower half of his face was covered by a thick beard of the same hue.

"You have done well, faithful Durok," Loki said and Durok noted that even the voice was different. It was deeper and far more masculine.

"I am afraid that the task you laid out for me has proven far more difficult than I had assumed. There is one called Lazarus Gray -- he and his companions have proven themselves to be worthy foes."

Loki shrugged. "My father and my brother are dead - they were truly 'worthy foes'. This Lazarus fellow may be impressive for a mortal, but he will be nothing more than a small trifle now that I am here."

"And then, my master?"

"Then this world will sink into the abyss... and it shall be the hand of Loki that crafts the world that will replace it!"

———— ∞ ————

In the dark recesses of his mind, a prisoner within his own flesh, lay the terrified remnants of Mike Simms.

CHAPTER VI
FOUR FOR MURDER!

A TALL BLONDE woman sat in the rear of the darkened bar, ignoring the stares of those around her. She wore a golden breastplate, tiara and wrist guards, along with a short white pleated skirt, greaves and sandals. All of these aside from her white sandals were trimmed in the same golden color that matched her breastplate. Her right hand was perched atop a shapely hip while her left rested atop the hilt of a sheathed sword. She towered over all the men in the room, standing well over six feet in height.

Her birth name was Violet Ray and she had been conceived in Serbia, shortly after the Great War. Nearly 16% of the nation's population had been killed during that awful conflict, leaving the nation in tatters.

A scientist by the name of James Axton, sickened by what he saw during the war, sought to find a way to ensure that it would never happen again. He felt that men had proven time and again to be too dangerous to rule -- he wanted to see a powerful woman in the position of ruler, one that wouldn't be swayed by the mad passions of the masculine mind.

Using a revolutionary scientific process of altering the glands and the chemicals they produced, he created a method of altering a human being to produce one that was stronger, smarter and better than nature could have ever intended. The only thing he lacked was a female subject -- which he found after touring one of the many orphanages in his homeland. He picked one that seemed suitable for the process, a skinny blonde girl that seemed possessed of a strong spirit. The glandular alterations led Violet to grow stronger and faster than any woman before her and her mind proved capable of making scientific leaps that defied explanation. She became not just the perfect woman... but the perfect human being! He dubbed her The Golden Amazon before he passed away and she now considered it her true name, far more than the one that had been given to her at the orphanage.

He died with a smile upon his face, knowing the good that he had done for the world. The day would come when she was ready to take her place as ruler of the entire planet but until then she occupied herself with battling those that would stand in her way. In recent months, that had meant fights with Nazis and even the strange Speaker from the Stars[5].

She had planned to leave Sovereign after the Speaker incident... she had identified The Black Terror as an appropriate mate, but he had spurned her attentions, instead choosing to remain loyal to Jean Starr. The sting of that rejection was still fresh... she had never experienced anything like it before.

Thoughts of The Black Terror had taken hold of her mind and she failed to notice that someone had taken the seat opposite hers. When she finally saw them, her eyes widened perceptibly.

"You were somewhere else entirely, weren't you?"

The Golden Amazon waved away the question, not interested in sharing any personal details with this man.

He was handsome, with well-sculpted features and piercing blue eyes. He wore a black shirt and slacks with a red tie, emblazoned with a tiny swastika tiepin. With the rising tensions in Europe, there were many that looked upon that swastika with disgust, but this fellow obviously didn't care for those opinions.

His name as Paul Alfred Müller-Murnau but he was known to Assistance Unlimited by another name: Nemesis.

Nemesis was the result of a complication mystic ritual that had imprinted all of Lazarus Gray's skills onto another man. While this transformed Müller-Murnau into a dark mirror image of Lazarus, it also eradicated all traces of the man he had once been. In fact, Müller-Murnau was very possibly not even his real identity... his fingerprints were known to no agency on earth and there was no history of anyone with that name until he'd shown up in Sovereign City, on the very same night that Richard

5 This is a modified version of The Golden Amazon's actual origin, as crafted by John R. Fearn. She teamed up with Assistance Unlimited to battle The Speaker from the Stars in volume 8.

Winthrop had become Lazarus Gray. Nemesis had used his versatile abilities to rise to two positions of power in just over half a decade: he had been the President of a bank and also the head of one of the largest German-American Bund organizations in the nation. He had finally realized his true purpose as Gray's opposite number and turned to a life of crime, allying himself first with the ancient Egyptian named Princess Femi and later with his own twisted version of Assistance Unlimited. It was during his imprisonment in Tartarus, the super-prison designed by Lazarus, that Nemesis had managed to cast his own spell, mystically impregnating Samantha Grace so that she could give birth to what he hoped would be the ubermensch. Since escaping from Tartarus, he had worked alongside a female Japanese warrior named Bushido and served as an agent of Germany's Occult Forces Project... that last appointment had led him to somewhat cross paths with The Golden Amazon, though not directly. He had unleashed The Speaker on Sovereign City and she had helped defeat it.

The Golden Amazon leaned forward, one hand drifting down to lay atop the hilt of her sword. "I came as you asked. Now tell me why I shouldn't paint these walls red with your blood."

Müller-Murnau seemed unperturbed by her threat. He crossed his legs and interlocked his fingers over his knee. "The Fuehrer's astrologer has prophesied a time of great danger... there are gods walking amongst us and humanity may not survive the next few weeks."

"The greatest threat to this world is Hitler himself," The Golden Amazon said dismissively. "He's a lunatic. The fact that you can sit there with a straight face and tell me that his astrologer is giving him direction says it all."

"The Fuehrer has his faults, but I would not qualify him as a lunatic."

"Then perhaps you're just as crazy as he is."

"I didn't come here to try and recruit you to the Reich," Nemesis said tersely. "So, may we please move on from the topic of the Fuehrer's sanity?"

"I'm still waiting to hear why I shouldn't skewer you."

"Bloodthirsty, aren't you?" Nemesis pursed his lips thoughtfully and then said, "The unrest will provide us with an opportunity to further our individual agendas. You want to eventually take over the world, yes? Well, I want to destroy Lazarus Gray. There's no reason why we can't work together on those goals."

"Why would I help you destroy Lazarus? He assisted me against The Speaker from the Stars."

"Because eventually he'll stand between you and your position as Empress of the world. No matter how much you think you'd be a fair and just ruler, the fact is that Lazarus and his friends won't agree. You know that. You may like them now but there will come a day when you'll have to deal with them."

The Golden Amazon sighed and looked away. She knew that Nemesis was right, and that knowledge was like a pinprick on her heart. Was it really The Black Terror that had brought her low like this? Never before has she felt weakness when it came to her mission... but now she was hesitant to slay men and women that stood between her and her destiny. This kind of foolishness could get worse the longer she allowed it to fester so there was only one way to deal with it, no matter how distasteful it seemed. "I am willing to consider allying myself with you - solely for the duration of the time it takes to remove Assistance Unlimited from my path. You will need to keep this in mind, however -- I do not take orders from you and the second I think that you are also a thorn to be removed from my side, I will gut you like a pig."

"I would expect nothing less," Nemesis replied. He held out a hand and The Golden Amazon looked at it for a moment before she reluctantly accepted it. She gripped it with all her strength, enjoying the expression of pain that he was unable to hide. The bones in his hand weren't broken but the ache would last for days.

When she released her hold on his hand, both of them rose simultaneously. He gestured for her to follow him and they departed the bar, ignoring the open-mouthed stares of their fellow patrons.

"I suppose you know that I've led my own version of Assistance Unlimited," he said as they stepped into a dark alleyway located between the bar and a Chinese-run laundromat.

"The absurdly named Murder Unlimited? Yes, I'm familiar with it." The Golden Amazon paused for a moment before quickly drawing her sword. They were not alone -- two people, a man and a woman, were stepping into view at the other end of the alley. They began approaching, leading The Golden Amazon to ask Nemesis, "Are they part of your team?"

"They are," Nemesis confirmed. "So, you can put away your weapon."

The Golden Amazon sheathed her sword and watched as the duo moved into view. Because of her study of Sovereign City and its champions, she was familiar with both.

Sayaka Kanda, the onna-bugeisha that went by the name Bushido, caught her eye first. She was beautiful, in a rather severe sort of fashion -- she had a perfectly shaped face and a lean, athletic body. She wore lightweight armor that somehow managed to emphasize rather than hide her lithe figure. In her right hand she held a naginata, a weapon whose length helped her when facing male opponents, many of whom had the advantages of size and strength. The naginata's blade was obviously very sharp and it gleamed in the light of a nearby streetlamp.

The two women regarded each other silently for a moment. The Golden Amazon was certain that Bushido was doing the same thing she was - sizing her up as a potential enemy.

When she turned her attention towards the man, she couldn't hide her surprise. The man wore a black bodysuit and hood with white gloves and boots. His face was hidden behind a skull-like mask and several guns were holstered at various points on his body - one at each hip plus a third housed on a shoulder holster on the left side of his body.

This man was Jakob Sporrenberg, a former Nazi soldier that had defected to America when he'd come to realize the full scope of Hitler's plans. He'd undergone a terrifying ordeal in which his outlook on life had been altered forever and after a tutelage at the hands of a vigilante known as The Darkling, Jakob had adopted the identify of Eidolon. As such, he'd been a member of Assistance Unlimited, leaving only when his methods were deemed excessive by Lazarus Gray.

"How do you know you can trust him?" The Golden Amazon asked Nemesis, gesturing towards Eidolon with one hand. "If I were Lazarus, I'd love to have a spy in your group."

Eidolon spoke up before Nemesis, saying, "I can speak for myself, thanks. I've done a lot of soul-searching over the last few months and I've realized that the only way to truly eradicate evil is to put it six feet underground. Lazarus has become an unwitting aid to the status quo -- he thinks that locking criminals up in Tartarus makes the city safer. He's wrong. It's just another turnstile that lets people like Nemesis go in and then come back out again. No offense," he added, directing his words at Müller-Murnau. When the Nazi gave a shrug, Eidolon continued. "I'm not happy to say this but this cesspool of a city is never going to get cleaned up until people like Lazarus are out of the way. Since I'll never be able to convince him to see things my way, there's only one real option. As much I dislike Nemesis, it makes sense to work together for now... once we've all gotten what we want, we can sort out the details afterward."

Nemesis caught Bushido's eye. The Japanese woman was obviously not certain about the wisdom of this grouping, but they had been over all of this before. The Golden Amazon and Eidolon were risky recruits but the potential for success was undeniable. There would have to be compromises, of course... both of these newcomers had certain moral standards that differed from those of Bushido and Nemesis but Müller-Murnau was confident that it could work.

"Anybody else joining or is it just us?" Eidolon asked.

"I think four is more than adequate," Nemesis replied. He smiled and added, "We have access to weaponry and materials that defy explanation... it's better to simply show you. If you come with me, you'll see that I have a pretty good idea about what Hitler's astrologer has foreseen... and the damage that will ensue will be partially by *our* hands!"

CHAPTER VII
DEAD MAN'S BOUNTY

"**G**EE WHIZ, BOB -- this place is a pigsty!"

The Black Terror silently agreed with his young ward's assessment though he thought about pointing out that the dead man's apartment had been ransacked by Durok's men so it wasn't fair to judge its current condition as being indicative of how John Watkins may have lived.

Tim Roland looked like a miniature version of his mentor, right down to wearing a matching version of Bob's Black Terror costume. Like Bob, he was an artificial human that had been implanted with false memories. Unlike Bob, he was unaware of his true nature. His optimistic nature was essential to keeping Bob out of his occasional dark-tempered funks.

Together, they had been dubbed The Terror Twins by the press. Tim wasn't an official member of Assistance Unlimited, but Bob often brought him along on excursions - partly for his own selfish reasons but also to placate the youth's constant yearning to be part of the team.

"Look for clues," Bob reminded his partner.

"Oh, I am -- I just wanted to point out that the next time you tell me to clean my room, I've never had this much of a mess!"

"I'll keep that in mind." Bob stepped over papers and overturned furniture, making his way to the dead man's bedroom. Police had already gone over the crime scene, but they had done so with their customary skill... meaning, they'd done a half-assed job of it. Bob could count the number of honest cops in Sovereign on two hands -- of course, that was an improvement over just a couple of years ago, when one hand would have been sufficient to number them.

Lazarus and the others from the museum had returned

with tales of strange warriors and disappearing men -- and the supposed hammer of Thor, wrapped up in heavy cloth. They'd listened with interest to Bob and Abby's tale of Baldr's death, which seemed to lend confirmation that they were in the midst of some form of Ragnarok.

Bob had gotten permission from Lazarus to come to John's apartment but not even Bob was really certain what it was he thought he might find. He still thought here had to be more to John's final weeks and months than what they'd known to this point... and Bob was certain that whatever that information might be would prove useful.

He found the man's sleeping quarters to be just as messy as the rest of the apartment. Curiously, however, the bed was untouched. It hadn't been made up, but the mattress was where it was supposed to be, and the sheets hadn't been pulled off. Given the poor state of the rest of the home, it struck Bob as quite strange.

Gripping the mattress with one hand, he tossed it aside with ease. On the floor was revealed a small wooden box, about a foot long and less than a foot in height. Because of the way the bedframe held the mattress up off the carpet, the box had been completely hidden from sight before Bob had revealed it.

"Gosh. How come the murderers and the cops didn't find that?" Tim asked, stepping up beside his mentor.

The Black Terror knelt and extended one gloved hand towards the box. The air rippled wherever his fingers touched, revealed an almost invisible covering over the floor. "Magic," he whispered. "I think what we're seeing is the fading remnants of a spell. If we'd come here yesterday, neither of us would be seeing anything at all. The creatures that killed John -- and our friends in blue -- didn't find it because they couldn't *see* it."

"Think you can open it?" Tim asked.

"Only way to find out." The Black Terror pushed his hand forward until he made contact with the lid of the box. The air felt so thick that it was like pushing through gelatin, but Bob's prodigious strength wasn't going to be denied.

When he touched the lid, the invisible field crackled and then vanished completely. The Black Terror allowed his fingers to close around the lip of the box's lid and he turned his head to smile at Tim. The young man was watching him with an excited gleam in his eyes. "Ready, chum?"

Tim slammed a fist into the palm of his other hand. "Boy, am I! Don't keep me in suspense, BT!"

The Black Terror opened the box, his eyes widening as he saw the stack of papers and photographs inside. It took a moment for the full meaning of all of it to sink in but when it did, he knew that his hunch had been right: this apartment held important secrets. "We need to get this back to Robeson Avenue," he said.

—⁂—

TIGGER PURRED LOUDLY as Samantha ran her fingers down his spine. The cat arched his back, chattering as she stroked his tail. "He's a little sweetie," Samantha said.

"Don't let him fool you," Sally said from the other room. "He'll make you think he's enjoying it and then he'll scratch you and run away."

Samantha grinned, thinking that sounded like almost every cat she'd ever known. It had been decided that Sally should stay at the team's headquarters for at least a couple of days, but Sally had insisted on returning home to get a few personal items, some clothing and to check on Tigger.

Sally returned to the room with a couple of small suitcases in tow. The young woman looked a little calmer than she had when Samantha had first met her, but her eyes were still a bit wild. "How do you do it?" she asked, setting the bags down on the floor.

"Do what?" Samantha asked, sitting back on the couch as Tigger rushed over to greet his mistress. Sally picked up the tomcat and scratched under his chin.

"You're a mom, right? How can you deal with all... this? Aren't you terrified that your daughter is going to be in danger?"

"Of course... but I see being part of Assistance Unlimited like others might view being a police officer or a soldier. It's dangerous but important work. My daughter is probably safer at Robeson Avenue than she would be anywhere else... when I can't be with her, she's watched over by martial arts masters, a witch, or a superhuman strongman." Sally seemed to consider that, but she seemed unconvinced. "And yes," Samantha said, "I know that she's also more likely to be a target because of my connection to Lazarus and the others... but that's a price I've decided I'm willing to pay, both for her and for myself."

After letting Tigger drop to the floor, Sally ran a hand through her hair and offered up a smile. "It's funny -- before I moved to Sovereign, I used to fantasize about meeting people like you and getting caught up in one of the adventures that I'd read about in the papers. Now that I'm involved in one, I keep wishing things would go back to normal."

"Sounds like a pretty common reaction to me," Samantha replied. She stood up and stretched, humorously reminding Sally of Tigger. Samantha moved to pick up one of Sally's suitcases. "If you want to bring kitty boy with you, that's fine."

"If you think I can come back to check on him tomorrow, I think he'd probably be happier at home."

Samantha's response was cut off by a knocking at the apartment's door. She held up a hand, warning Sally to keep quiet, and reached under her own skirt to unholster her pistol. After setting Sally's bag on the couch, she approached the door and put her eye up to the peephole. There was no one to be seen on the other side. "Who is it?" she asked, remembering Sally's description of the previous night's event. Was it Durok and his minions again?

A whippet-thin figure moved into view. He wore a long overcoat with an upturned collar and a small cigarette dangled between his lips. He reached up with a thin hand to remove the smoke, asking, "Samantha? That you?"

With a sigh, Samantha put her pistol away and unlocked the door. She knew Inspector Cord very well -- in fact, they'd dated until just before she'd given birth to Emily. Cord claimed to trust her, but he'd had a very hard time accepting that she hadn't cheated on him and that the pregnancy had been mystically induced. Samantha knew how absurd it sounded but she also believed that he should have trusted her, no matter out how outlandish it seemed.

"Inspector," she said frostily. She positioned her body in the doorway, preventing him from entering. "To what do we owe the pleasure?"

"Miss Grace," he answered, no longer referring to her by her first name since she'd greeted him in an impersonal manner. "Is Miss Weatherby here?"

"She is. What do you need her for?"

"I wanted to ask her a few questions related to the Watkins murder. She had an appointment with him for lunch today, didn't she?"

"You know that she did," Samantha answered. "She's under our protection and I'm sure that we'll crack the case before you even sniff the first clue - as usual."

Insulting his police work was a bit too much for Cord and he jabbed in her direction with his cigarette. "Don't get all high-and-mighty with me! I've greased the wheels for your boss too many times to count!"

Both of them looked down the hall as the elevator dinged and the doors slid open. A large man wearing furs and leathers stepped out of the lift. Most of his head was hidden beneath a metal helm topped by curved horns. In his right hand was a massive war club that was dripping with blood. Samantha immediately suspected that there was a dead elevator attendant still in the lift.

Whatever their differences, Cord and Samantha put them all aside for the moment. The Inspector turned to face the big man who was now striding towards them. "Take Miss Weatherby down with the fire escape," he said, reaching under his coat to draw out a service revolver. "I'll slow this brute down."

Samantha was pretty certain that she could hold off the warrior better than Cord could, but she also knew that there might be more threats outside -- and her priority was protecting Sally. So instead of arguing, she turned back inside and shoved the door closed, locking both the small lock and the deadbolt. "Out the window!" she shouted, startling Sally. The young woman recovered quickly and both of them were out the window in less than a minute, abandoning both suitcases. Tigger bolted under the couch, out of sight.

"What's going on?" Sally asked as she followed Samantha down the fire escape. They were only a few floors up, but her heels made running difficult, so she paused to take off her shoes.

She held one in each hand as they descended to the ground.

"They're still after you. I'm not sure why." Samantha seized Sally by the elbow and pulled the terrified woman toward her parked car.

"Maybe they think I still have the pendant?"

"Shouldn't be important any longer - Durok knows we have the hammer!" Samantha shoved Sally forward as they reached the parking lot. "Get in!" she shouted.

Sally ran around to the other side of the car and got into the passenger seat, clutching her chest with one hand.

Samantha yanked open the driver's side door and was about to slide behind the wheel when Sally's gasp made her pause with her body halfway in the car.

Turning back toward the building, she saw the helmeted warrior silhouetted in the open window of Sally's apartment. The man was holding something over his head, hefting it like a man-sized bag of potatoes. She knew instinctively what it was, and the knowledge hit in the heart like a dagger's edge.

The warrior threw the object with all his strength and both women clearly saw that it was a human body as it hurtled towards the street below.

Inspector Cord struck the ground with a sickening sound, his bones shattering upon impact. Samantha could only hope that he was already dead before he landed and that he hadn't suffered too much. An oncoming car failed to swerve out of the way and its tires rattled as the vehicle ran over Cord's body.

The warrior leaned out of the window and bellowed, "You can run but you cannot hide, Thrúd! Your uncle shall find you! You won't escape from him again!"

Samantha had heard enough. She slammed her door shut and started the engine, immediately shifting gears. She burned rubber as her automobile rocketed into traffic, causing several other vehicles to slam on their brakes and honk their horns.

With warm tears beginning to stream down her face, Samantha directed her car towards home. She knew that Sally was asking questions, but she couldn't hear them over the pounding of her own heart.

Cord was dead... he'd put his life on the line to try and protect her and Sally.

"You stupid bastard," she whispered.

CHAPTER VIII
THE THUNDER GOD'S DAUGHTER

LAZARUS SAT ALONE in his private office, located on the same floor as the quarters he shared with Kelly and their son, Ezekiel. Downstairs, he knew that the others were reacting in various ways to the news of Cord's death... and even those that weren't particularly fond of the man knew of his importance to Samantha, so they, too, were in a somber mood.

Dark thoughts were plaguing the leader of Assistance Unlimited. On the desk in front of him were a variety of photographs and papers brought to him by The Black Terror... and a small notepad next to these had a single word scribbled on the top page: Thrúd.

Bob's discovery cast several things in a new light. The photographs were of Sally at various stages of her life, most of them clipped from newspaper articles - one showed her and her second grade class on a field trip, another was of her receiving a certificate for placing first in a local essay contest during her sixth grade year. The rest were similar in nature, with one or two being candid images taken from a good distance away. John's bumping into her had hardly been the accidental event that it had seemed... he knew who she was, and he knew her daily schedule. Furthermore, he had not dropped the pendant by chance at all -- he had done knowing that she would pick it up.

The 'why' of it all was the truly interesting thing -- and the shouted warning from the man that killed Cord held the key, Lazarus believed. He had yelled out the name Thrúd... and Lazarus had looked in a volume on Norse mythology to discover that Thrúd was the daughter of Thor and the warrior goddess, Sif.

He also thought about Duroks words to him during their

battle -- that his spirit would be grafted onto a new body. Presumably, that had already happened by now. Lazarus was now wondering if something similar might have happen with Thrúd... what if, to hide her from their enemies or to simply keep her away from the war threatening Asgard, Thor and Sif had placed their daughter's spirit in a human form? If so, Thrúd might have grown up in the world of mortals, never knowing her true origins.

Lazarus was now suspecting that Sally Weatherby was, in fact, that daughter. If so, she was the heir to her father's weapon... the mighty hammer was rightfully hers. Of course, at present her timid nature made her unlikely to be an accomplished warrior... but Lazarus suspected that her heritage might come to the fore if and when she made physical contact with the hammer.

Rising from his seat, Lazarus wandered over to a locked cabinet. He retrieved a key from his pocket and opened it, revealing the cloth-covered form of Mjölnir. He had discovered that he could only lift the object by wrapping it in something else. If he didn't do this, Mjölnir was too heavy to lift. Kelly had told him that were some myths that implied that only one deemed worthy by the hammer itself could utilize the powerful weapon. Lazarus was fairly certain that Sally would find it easy to do.

He reached in and removed the hammer, making sure to keep the cloth over the artifact's surface. Even through the cloth, he could feel the weight of ages... this was not just some mystical artifact, it was a holy one. Men and women around the world had sought protection by wearing sigils in its image and even now the mention of 'Thor's hammer' would be enough to excite the hearts and minds of adventure lovers the world over.

Knowing that the time had come, Lazarus set the hammer atop the papers on his desk and then pressed a button on a small control panel located on the wall beside the door. "Miss Weatherby, could you please come to my office? I'm sure one of the team can show you the way."

Casting his eyes back to Mjölnir, Lazarus couldn't help but wonder why his life had become entwined with Norse mythology. Just a few years back, he had teamed with The Peregrine and Gravedigger to defeat the Mother of Pus in a series of events that they had collectively dubbed Götterdämmerung[6] -- now, with the actual Ragnarok bearing down upon them, it appeared that perhaps they had indulged in too much hyperbole.

⁂

SALLY HAD HOPED that Eun would be the one to escort her to see Lazarus, but she wasn't altogether unhappy that Morgan Watts had jumped at the opportunity. True, he was old enough to be her father, but he was also quite dapper and treated her like she was a princess -- which, given how stressful the past couple of days had been, was not unwelcome.

Besides, Eun had seemed to be completely unfazed by her attempts at conversation... perhaps she simply wasn't his type?

Look at me, she mused. *Worrying over a man's attention -- or lack thereof -- when another fellow that I was crushing on has ended up dead! Hopefully it's just my way of coping with all this craziness... better to worry about my love life than concentrate on people that want to harm me.*

"You're perfectly safe here," Morgan said gently. He reached out to take her hand and gave it a squeeze before releasing it. Sally smiled in reply, remembering that she'd read somewhere that Morgan had once been a criminal before turning over a new leaf as a member of Assistance Unlimited. It was hard to picture him as a 'bad guy.' His pencil-thin mustache was perfectly trimmed, his suit fit him impeccably and he smelled like expensive cologne.

"Thank you, Morgan. I appreciate the kindness all of you have shown me -- especially in light of the fact that I don't have any money to pay you with."

"Like we told you, payment is nice -- it's not cheap keeping an operation like this running -- but in the end, none of us are doing this for the money."

Sally nodded, having seen enough to know that he wasn't just blowing smoke up her skirt. "Do you have any children, Morgan?"

"No... never quite found the right woman to settle down with. I got hitched a while back, but it turned out to be a pack

---

6 As told in the novel called, you guessed it, *Götterdämmerung.*

of lies so it was annulled. I did pop the question to somebody a little after that, but she said no[7]."

"Well, that's a shame. I think you'd have made a great father."

Sally instantly regretted her words because she saw look of disappointment pass over Morgan's face. She realized that perhaps his interest in her hadn't been as paternal as she'd assumed... and she'd just insulted him by drawing attention to their age difference."

Morgan stopped outside of Lazarus Gray's office. "Go on in," he said.

"I -- I want to apologize if I..."

Morgan brushed aside her apology by giving a shake of his head and opening the door for her. She saw Lazarus standing next to his desk, a bundle of cloth in front of him. When she looked back at Morgan, he was already halfway down the hall.

I'M A DAMNED *fool*.

Morgan paused in front of the elevator, reaching up to smooth out his mustache. He had to face facts - he was more likely to make young women picture him as a father figure than as a potential suitor.

He'd wasted too many of his prime years chasing after women that weren't the type to bring home to mother. Now that he wanted to settle down, he desired a different sort of female... but there was a major problem: he had gotten older but the women he fancied were still just as young as ever.

"Don't take this the wrong way but maybe you should look at women your own age."

Morgan whirled about and saw Abby watching him with a concerned expression. He started to pretend that he didn't know what she was talking about, but he finally sighed, seeing no point in denying it. "You saw all that, did you?"

"I did. I came up to check on the kids for Kelly... They're listening to *Terry and the Pirates*."

"They're too little to follow it," Morgan replied.

"Doesn't matter. They both love it." Abby moved closer and

7 Both of those events took place in our last volume.

lowered her voice. "You're getting older. Doesn't mean you're doomed to being alone forever."

"Easy for you to say. You're in full bloom."

"Well, thank you! But my petals aren't as rosy as they used to be." Abby slipped her arm in his and stepped into the elevator carriage when the doors opened. "Kelly's going to relieve me as the babysitter so why don't I buy you a drink?"

Morgan grinned despite himself. "I could never say no to a pretty woman."

ꙮ

SALLY FELT UNCOMFORTABLE under the gaze of Lazarus Gray. He had asked her to take a seat upon entering and since then he had remained silent, obviously trying to decide how to broach a difficult subject. Sally's eyes kept going back to the object that lay under the cloth on his desk… and to the photographs and newspaper clippings that lay underneath that. Were those pictures of her?

"Have you ever felt like you were living a lie, Miss Weatherby?"

"Excuse me?"

"Did you ever feel like you were destined for greater things?"

"I suppose so… doesn't everyone, though? I remember reading about Sovereign City and its heroes when I was growing up. Sometimes I'd dream of being rescued by Doc Daye from a terrible villain or finding the clue that would allow him to best a spy ring. Then when Assistance Unlimited came around, my fantasies shifted -- suddenly I realized that I didn't have to be the one to be rescued… I could do the rescuing myself! Samantha Grace and then later Abigail Cross were both inspirations to me!"

Lazarus studied her, noting how her voice and features became more animated as she talked. She was so slight that it was hard to picture her as the daughter of Thor, but he knew that her present form did not necessarily reflect the steel that lay within her.

"I believe that you might the only one of us that might be able to use this." He leaned forward and pulled the cloth from Mjölnir, revealing the ancient weapon. He saw her eyes widen and he was certain that he saw a flicker of recognition. "Will you pick it up?"

"What is that?" she asked.

"What do you think it is?"

"I heard your friends talking about the hammer of Thor…"

"Does saying that Thunder God's name make you feel anything in particular?"

Sally shifted uncomfortably, her gaze never leaving the hammer. Her fingers were twitching, as if they wanted to reach out and seize the weapon but she was afraid to give in to the desire. "I… I don't know. I don't know what you're asking," she stammered.

"I believe that your true name is Thrúd," Lazarus said. He again saw a flinch of recognition though she said nothing in reply. Continuing, he said, "I believe that your mother and father sought to keep you safe by sending your soul to Midgard, the realm of mortals. I believe that your spirit ended up in the body of an infant named Sally Weatherby and I think that you might have lived out your entire life without learning the truth… but that John Watkins stumbled upon it while searching for the key to the hammer's box. I think that he knew his life was in danger and that he deliberately crossed paths with you so that you could gain the pendant and, eventually, use it to claim your birthright."

"That sounds crazy," Sally whispered but Lazarus knew that she was feeling the truth of his words.

"Then take the hammer and prove me wrong," he urged.

With a trembling hand, Sally did just that -- she reached out and allowed her fingertips to slide over the hammer's handle. As soon as she made contact with it, sparks of electricity raced along her hand and up her arm. It didn't seem to hurt her - in fact, she reacted not at all to the light display. Gripping the handle, she stood up and lifted Mjölnir off the desktop. She hefted it effortlessly, but Lazarus was less impressed by her feat of strength than he was by the transformation that seemed to occur almost simultaneously.

Sally Weatherby's body was covered in sparkling lights and crackling electricity. Her clothing was altered before Gray's eyes, shifting from a modern blouse and skirt to a metal breastplate, a furred loincloth that hung loosely between her thighs, knee-high boots comprised of leather and fur, a heavy cloak slung over one shoulder and a war helm that covered the upper half of her head. Her long red hair was now braided and hung down her back.

When she looked at Lazarus, Mjölnir gripped tightly in her right hand, she seemed taller and broader than before, though he wasn't sure if that was truly the case or simply an illusory result of her more regal bearing. "You have proven your wisdom, Lazarus Gray," she said, her speech pattern noticeably more formal. "No longer am I merely Sally Weatherby, though she still resides with me... my nature as the heir to the throne of Asgard has been confirmed."

Lazarus stepped around the desk, coming close to her. She not only looked different, she *smelled* different. Gone was her inexpensive but pleasant perfume scent - in its place she now smelled of fresh air and exotic spices.

"You're two minds in one?" Lazarus asked.

"Yes - I feel Sally Weatherby's mind within mine but we are different people... her soul and mine are intertwined but not the same." Thrúd began spinning the hammer in her grip and Lazarus felt the quality of the air begin to change: it was now causing his hair to stand on end. "We must check on the damage done to the golden realm!"

"Wait, what do you mean?"

What happened next brought an abrupt answer to that question: a rift in the air, the edges of which crackled with lightning, opened before them -- on the other side of the portal lay the shattered remains of the Bifrost bridge, the rainbow pathway that connected the various worlds to Asgard.

"By Odin's beard," Thrúd whispered. She lowered her head for a moment before stepping into the rift, her booted feet resting on a ragged edge of rainbow bridge. Lazarus moved to join her, and he smelled death and fire, carried on a wind that blew his silver-streaked hair.

In the distance both could see what was left of Asgard and it was not a pretty sight. The golden spires had been toppled and the bodies of the dead were piled upon one another, creating tiny mountains of rotting corpses. Flames danced here and there, laying final siege to an empire that had been ancient before humanity had crawled from the primordial sludge.

"My uncle betrayed us," Thrúd said. She held her father's hammer between her breasts, as if in its touch she could somehow reach across the void and feel her father's presence. "Sold us out to the forces of evil..."

"Loki was slain by Heimdall, wasn't he?" Lazarus asked.

"So, it is said but not every version of Ragnarok is like the previous... all of history is but a wheel, eternally turning." Thrúd whirled the might hammer and then tossed it forward without releasing her grip upon the handle. As she was pulled along by its power, she snatched up Lazarus by the hand. Lazarus felt his arm nearly wrench from its socket as Thrúd flew through the air. It wasn't true flight, of course, but the power of Mjölnir was enough to allow them to cleave through the skies.

They soared over the broken bridge and finally came to a gentle landing just shy of set of shattered marble stairs and a soaring, cathedral-like structure. The building's windows were all broken, and a headless corpse was lying half-in and half-out of the doorway. Whomever the man had been, his body was hacked up in a dozen different places and blood had pooled beneath his body.

Lazarus felt a sense of unreality being here, but he had been to Carcosa[8] and Hel[9]l itself so he had experience with unusual places. Looking around, he said, "I don't see anyone left alive."

Thrúd sighed and for the first time since her transformation Lazarus thought he saw some of Sally Weatherby in her. "I fear that I am the last of my family... No. No, that's not correct. Loki still lives, in one form or another. Of that, I am certain." Beneath her helm, her features twisted into an expression of grim resolve. "But he shall not live for much longer."

Lazarus looked at her and asked, "Do you know what Loki might be trying to do now? How will he try to destroy the earth?"

"According to the myths, Midgard shall sink into the oceans of creation... at which point, Loki - or whomever stands alone from the previous universe - could shape the next cycle as he or she saw fit. What that means in actual terms, I cannot say. The

8 See volume 7.
9 See volume 6.

'oceans of creation' might not be literal."

Something moving through the smoky sky caught Lazarus' eye and he pushed past Thrúd so he could get a better look at it. A zeppelin passed overhead, a massive airship emblazoned with a symbol on the side: it was an image of the globe, with a dagger shoved right through it. Despite the fact that he had never seen it before, Lazarus had little doubt about the meaning of that symbol... it spoke of men and women that sought to do harm to the entire planet if anyone stood in their way. Though their membership had varied greatly in their two previous incarnations, Lazarus had been afraid that they would return due to the fact that the leaders of the most recent version were still free.

"Murder Unlimited," he said aloud.

"They are mortals? But how did they come to be here?"

"I don't know but I guarantee you, nothing good's going to come of this."

Thrúd grinned. "Then let us bring them low so that we may question them!" She whirled Mjölnir over her head and then threw it with all of her Asgardian might. Lazarus heard it whistle through the air before it pierced the side of the zeppelin and continued on to the other side of the airship. The weapon continued along in an arc, turning back to return to its owner's hand.

The zeppelin began to lose altitude quickly and it faltered until crashing hard atop a golden-topped building.

Lazarus looked about but saw no way to reach that building's roof. He needed to know if Nemesis was inside that ship... had he been killed? If not, he had to save his life and put him back where he belonged -- in Tartarus.

Thrúd could read his thoughts on his face. She wrapped a hand around his waist and repeated the process that had allowed them to traverse the shattered bridge: she hurled Mjölnir and allowed them both to be pulled along in its wake.

Landing on the rooftop, Lazarus pulled away from her and approached the fallen zeppelin. Gas was spilling out into the air and he knew that it was extremely flammable -- with the fires raging throughout the city, he had only moments to rescue anyone that might be within the ship.

Without any fear for his own safety, Lazarus stepped within the airship. He gave no hesitation over the fact that the men and women within were most likely ones that wished to kill him in turn - they were human beings and if he could save their lives, he had to take the chance.

What he saw upon entering the zeppelin was not what he expected, however. There were three men, two of whom were obviously dead. They were strapped into chairs in the pilot's cabin, their necks at odd angles and blood dripping from their noses and mouths.

The third being in the airship looked shaken but otherwise unharmed -- it was a blonde woman whose hair was pulled back in a ponytail. She wore a white jumpsuit with red stripes along the arms and outer legs - it matched the ones worn by the dead pilots. On her left breast was a small patch bearing the Murder Unlimited symbol and strapped to her left hip was a dagger. She recognized Lazarus and uttered an oath in German before drawing her blade.

Speaking in fluent German, Lazarus warned, "We need to get you out of here -- the entire zeppelin could go up in flames!"

"Better to die than let you live another day," the woman snarled. Her lower lip was torn slightly from the crash landing and a thin trail of red was spreading down her pale white chin.

The woman brandished her blade with great skill, but Lazarus was her superior. He blocked the first swipe and then seized hold of her arm, yanking her towards him and then bringing his elbow down upon her forearm. The blow was enough to cause her to gasp in pain and lose her grip on the knife. It fell to the floor and Lazarus stomped his foot down on top of it before kicking it behind him. As he'd intended, the weapon went right out the makeshift entrance that had granted him access.

His foe was not finished, however - she slammed her head forward, catching Lazarus on his right temple. He grunted and she capitalized on his momentary distraction to drive her knee into his groin.

As Lazarus bent over in pain, the woman danced back a few steps. She rubbed her injured arm and said, "If I kill you, I'll be hailed as a hero back home..."

"By whom?" Lazarus asked between gritted teeth. "Nemesis?"

"He is a great man," she said, answering his question without meaning to.

"You're a member of Murder Unlimited?" he asked, dodging a kick aimed at his midsection. He grabbed her ankle as he moved past and shoved her off-balance. She caught herself against the wall, narrowly avoiding losing her feet.

"I serve them," the woman answered.

"How did you get here?"

Her response was to launch herself at him with her fingernails ready to rake his eyes out. Lazarus braced himself to catch her, but the action was not needed - for just then Mjölnir whistled through the air, slamming right into the woman's head. Her skull shattered upon impact, sending blood, hair and brains against the wall. Her corpse landed with a thud at Gray's feet.

Lazarus turned as Mjölnir returned to its mistress. Thrúd looked at him and either didn't pick up on his annoyance or wasn't concerned with it. "A fire has begun to creep up the side of this building. We have to leave it."

"I wanted to question her."

"There's no need. I can tell you how they found their way into Asgard. While you were fighting her, I was examining their vessel."

Lazarus bent down and examined the dead woman's body, finding a small notebook secreted in a rear pocket. He carried it with him as he followed Thrúd back outside the zeppelin. He saw that she was right - flames were beginning to encroach on their position and the entire rooftop would be soon caught up in a massive conflagration.

They said nothing to one another until Thrúd had borne him back to the ground and they were safely away from the scene. "You said you knew how they got here?" he prompted.

"They've been coming back and forth some time now - and with the city fallen, they've been looting it. I saw crates of weapons and artifacts in their cargo hold. And this is how they managed to traverse the realms." Thrúd held out a hand and in its palm, she held several small golden spheres, each adorned with gems of red and blue. "These are Portal Keys, used to allow mortal devices to survive the passage from your world to ours."

Lazarus frowned, his mind running through the possibilities.

If Nemesis had Asgardian items at his disposal, that was extremely bad. "We need to go back," he said and was relieved that Thrúd didn't seem willing to argue the point. He could only hope that the notebook he'd picked up might contain a clue as to where Murder Unlimited was hiding…

CHAPTER IX
A PLAGUE OF EVIL

666 HOLDER WAY was in the most despicable part of the city, which was saying something quite severe given the overall reputation of Sovereign. The streets were lined with prostitutes and drug pushers, along with mobsters that wore their guns openly. The few police officers that drove through the area were all on mob's payroll and turned a blind eye to the many crimes they saw taking place.

The brownstone located at this particular address was visibly decrepit. The windows were boarded up and there were bloodstains on the front steps. A cruelly lettered sign warned "No Trespassers" on the front door.

Few people knew that this structure had been the headquarters for the criminal enterprise known as Murder Unlimited. Since their most recent defeat, the area had been put under the watchful gaze of several police officers that were trusted by Inspector Cord… unfortunately, these men had been blackmailed by Bushido and so they had been turning a blind eye to the comings and goings at Holder Way.

Eun Jiwon sat in a dark sedan parked down the street from the shabby building. As soon as Lazarus had returned from Asgard, he'd asked for a volunteer to come and check on the villainous team's former headquarters - and Eun's hand had gone up faster than anyone else's. He and his boyfriend were in the middle of a spat so he knew they wouldn't be spending the night together and the best way that Eun had found to get over an aching heart was to smash someone's face in.

Since he'd arrived fifteen minutes ago, he'd seen absolutely no activity at 666 Holder Way. He did notice that the prostitutes gave the place a wide berth - not a single one of them was selling their wares in front of that ghoulish location. He didn't blame them - it was so foul looking that he thought it would kill any man's erection... of course, he'd been inside the place and knew that for all its exterior blemishes, it was quite the opposite within.

No way they're still operating out of this place, he thought as he slipped around back. *Nemesis is almost as smart as Lazarus and he'd know that we'd come looking for him here, so he's got to be somewhere else.*

Still, Eun was prepared to be as stealthy and careful as possible. He'd learned the hard way to never assume too much when it came to the criminal element. Some of them simply didn't think the way a normal person would.

The back door was covered by a hand-painted sign that read NO ADMITTANCE but Eun ignored it, reaching for the knob and giving it a twist. To his surprise, it swung open with ease, emitting only the tiniest of squeaks.

Slipping inside, Eun saw that he was entering into a small hallway that led into a pantry and kitchen. He passed through these, pausing only long enough to assure himself that it had not been recently used -- aside from rat droppings, he didn't see anything that suggested anything living had been here in months.

Frowning, Eun was wondering if he should bother checking out the rest of the building - this was a waste of his time. It made more sense to go shake down a few members of the criminal element and see if anybody had heard tell of Murder Unlimited's reformation. If they were hiring people to work for them and had the capital to afford a zeppelin, then there was bound to be talk.

"I figured one of you would come by here."

Eun froze in place, amazed and more than a little bit embarrassed that someone could have gotten the drop on him. He whirled about, seeing a shadowy figure in the corner of the kitchen... but he relaxed when he recognized the masked personage of Eidolon.

"Jakob," Eun said, straightening up. "Guess you're here for the same reason I am, eh?"

"What reason would that be?"

"Murder Unlimited."

Eidolon gave a small nod. "Yeah, actually… Murder Unlimited *is* why I'm here." To Eun's surprise, his former teammate drew a pistol and pointed it at him. "Hate to do this."

Eun's eyes widened. "Jakob…?"

Eidolon fired three times.

— ⁂ —

NEMESIS AND BUSHIDO were more than partners in crime… they were lovers and soon to be parents. The Japanese woman was not showing it, but she was quite pregnant - her child would be the perfect union of an Aryan superman and Asia's greatest female warrior.

As she crouched low, slowing swinging her weapon in a graceful arc, she was pleased to find that a search of her emotions yielded nothing close to 'love' for Müller-Murnau. She respected him and felt that the two of them made for a powerful team but thankfully the weakness that came from romantic love had not affected her.

These practice sessions were essential to maintaining her fitness and clarity of mind. Their current scheme was one that seemed destined for success… and once Lazarus Gray was defeated, she was going to return to her homeland to give birth. She would turn their child over to the Emperor to be raised as he saw fit and then she hoped to be given leave to travel back to America where she could continue working alongside Nemesis.

She heard the front door of the team's penthouse apartment open and close. From the tread of the footsteps she knew that it was Eidolon returning. Despite the Golden Amazon's suspicions about Jakob Sporrenberg, Bushido believed the German when he said he saw the necessity of killing Lazarus. Of course, he was a traitor twice over having betrayed not only Assistance Unlimited but also The Fuehrer himself… so he would be watched carefully, just in case.

Straightening, she saw Eidolon pass by her room, and she stopped him with a word of greeting. When he paused, she added, "The zeppelin didn't return. Nemesis is prepping a group to go and investigate."

Eidolon gave a shrug. "No telling what happened... anything from a mechanical failure to some Asgardian beast attacking them."

Bushido switched subjects without warning, asking, "Did your 'hunch' bear fruit?"

"It did, actually. I was about to give up when one of Assistance Unlimited showed up at Holder Way. It was Eun Jiwon."

"An honorable fighter. What happened?"

"I shot him."

"He's dead?"

"I didn't stay to watch him bleed out but he was in no shape to go and get help so I'd say by now... the answer to that would be yes."

"And you are fine with that? With killing a man you used to call friend?"

"I wouldn't say I'm fine with it -- but it's something that had to be done." Eidolon started to move away, headed towards the large room at the end of the hall. "Is Nemesis in his quarters?"

"He is."

Bushido watched as the German stopped outside her lover's door, knocking quickly. When Nemesis appeared, opening the door to let Eidolon enter, she caught his eye, and something passed between them... a look of warning. If Eun had been alone, there would have been no reason not to ensure his demise... she wondered if Eidolon had even shot him at all.

───── ✖✖✖ ─────

DR. HANCOCK GRIMACED as he took a step away from the young man on the gurney. The members of Assistance Unlimited were waiting for him outside the team's medical area and he wished that he had better news for them. The best he could say at this point was that Eun was not dead... it was so close, however, that he felt like he'd be giving Lazarus false hope by saying so.

Of all the team, he liked Eun and Bob the best... Bob because he was a chemist and they had things to talk about. With Eun, it was a recent development - the two men had shared an adventure last year, one that had nearly left Hancock an invalid.

That shared experience meant that he and Eun now shared a powerful bond.

"Come in!" Hancock shouted and the door opened to reveal the concerned faces of Eun's teammates. They moved into the room, allowing Lazarus to take the lead - the so-called daughter of Thor was not present, however. She had stepped out onto the roof of the building, saying she wanted to commune with the night air.

Samantha had called Eun's boyfriend and he was en route but due to the nature of Eun's injuries, no one wanted to wait for him before hearing the details.

"Is he going to live?" Lazarus asked.

"It's touch and go," Hancock admitted. "Whoever placed that call to headquarters definitely saved his life... if you hadn't gotten to him when you did, he'd have bled out."

Lazarus nodded... the anonymous phone call had been placed from one of the payphones located in a pharmacy down the street from 666 Holder Way. No one in the establishment saw who had placed the call -- or they simply weren't willing to give up the information. "Tell us more, doctor."

"All three bullets are lodged inside his body and need to be removed. He's incredibly lucky - a inch more in either direction and he'd have been killed on the spot. Even so, the surgery is going to require a steady hand."

"Lucky," Lazarus murmured. "Doctor, can you perform the surgery here or should we have him transported to Sovereign General?"

"I can do it here. I've already put a call in to a couple of nurses that can assist me."

"Good. Let me know what you need -- and doctor?"

"Yes?"

"When you get those bullets out of him, I want to see them."

Morgan, standing at his friend's side, asked quietly, "You've got a suspicion, don't you?"

"I do," Lazarus admitted. "It may not have been luck at all that saved Eun's life. I think it might have been skill... and if so, there's only so many men on earth that could have pulled it off."

M ÜLLER-MURNAU STOOD BY a table topped by relics of another world: weapons, leather-bound books and things that no one present had been able to identify yet. "So, you left him to die?" he asked in German.

Eidolon nodded. He had removed his skull, revealing a face that was quite handsome but glistening with sweat. "I would have put another bullet in him to make sure, but I was out of ammunition."

"Inconvenient," Nemesis replied, lifting up a spear topped by some sort of bluish-silver metal that he'd never seen before. "I'm surprised you'd be so careless - did it take that many shots to hit him?"

"No," Jakob said, bristling a bit at the unspoken accusation. "I had gone hunting for criminals last night and made the mistake of thinking I'd reloaded this morning. Obviously, I hadn't."

"Obviously." Nemesis set the spear down and regarded Eidolon with a steely smile. "I need you to be a good soldier, Jakob... the sort you were before you left Germany. I have to be able to trust you. Assistance Unlimited, as you well know, is a well-oiled machine. They follow Lazarus Gray without hesitation and, in turn, he knows that they will do exactly as they promise they will. If we can't say the same for one another, we're going to lose -- and it doesn't matter how many Asgardian weapons we have."

Jakob sighed and gave a nod. "You're right... but you can trust me. Lazarus kicked me out because I refused to be his lapdog. I'm not loyal to him anymore."

"What about Abigail? The two of you were lovers, weren't you? Do you think you could kill her if you had to?"

Jakob looked directly into the eyes of Nemesis and he said in an emotionless voice, "If she crosses my path, I'd give her one chance to join us. If she refused -- and I'm sure she would -- then whatever happens next is her own fault."

Nemesis stared at him for a long moment and when he finally spoke, his words were accompanied by a smile. "Good man, Jakob." He looked back to the weapons and other artifacts. "I'm breaking a sworn oath by keeping these for myself."

"To the OFP?" Eidolon asked.

Nemesis nodded. The Occult Forces Project, known as Geheimnisvolles Kraft-Projekt in German, was a subset of The Ahnenerbe and was dedicated to utilizing super-science and magic in the name of The Reich. The group had achieved several notable successes when it came to creating larger-than-life figures to spread the Nazi ideals across the globe and was constantly on the look-out for occult power. "Yes," he said. "It was the OFP that sent me the Portal Keys to try and decipher. They found them in the ruins of a golden chariot that appeared over the skies of Baden-Wurttemberg before crashing in the Black Forest. It took me several weeks to discover that they could open a gateway to the home of the gods."

"And you haven't told the OFP about it," Eidolon said, understanding where all this was going. "If they find out, they'll liquidate you and take all of this for the Reich."

"By the time they're aware of my deception, it will be too late." Nemesis looked at Jakob and his eyes flashed with *something* -- madness? a sense of divine purpose? Jakob wasn't sure. "I've always been destined for greatness, Jakob. That's why I was chosen for the Nemesis project... why I made a child with Samantha that will be destined for great things... and why those Portal Keys ended up in my hands and not someone else."

"What's the endgame here? I know you want to kill Lazarus... but after that, I'm assuming you're not going to use all of this Asgardian stuff to help Hitler win the war... Are you?"

"No, I'm not. I'm loyal to the Fuehrer's agenda but not to the man himself... not when I'm better suited for ruling than he ever would be. I'd like to give him a place of honor in my new world order but if he refuses, I'll simply have to remove him completely." Nemesis looked at Jakob and his eyes suddenly darkened until they were completely black. When he spoke again, his voice was much darker than before, and Jakob shifted uncomfortably every time the man's tongue came into view - it was too big, too thick... and covered with greenish scales. "I've eaten of several pieces of fruit that came from Asgard, Jakob. They've been changing me. I can hide it when I want -- for now. Eventually, I won't be able to do, though. I'm becoming something more and less than human. Nobody will be able to call me a copy of Lazarus Gray any longer."

HE GOLDEN AMAZON fingered the circlet that Nemesis had given her. She was alone with the object in her sparsely furnished room and she reclined on her bed. She was nude, her weapons and armor splayed on the floor. The circle was made to fit around her neck and it was silvery-white in color. A magical charm had been placed on the object, which gave it the ability to increase the density of its wearer's flesh. For the Golden Amazon, this meant that her already powerful defenses were enhanced to the point where small-caliber bullets would bounce right off of her.

The gift did not come without strings, of course. Nemesis had offered to her with words of friendship, but she knew that accepting it meant that she was bound by honor to remain true to him... but ultimately, she would not hesitate to betray him if necessary. Her only real loyalty was to herself and her mission... as long as the rest of Murder Unlimited allowed her to pursue her goals, she would do whatever they asked in service to their own agenda. The day would inevitably come when those goals would diverge, however, and at that point the circlet would be a boon to her and a curse to her enemies.

She heard footsteps outside of her door and she slid the circlet around her neck even as she sat up. When the knocking came a second later, she reached down and snatched up her sword. Holding the weapon down at her side, she approached the door and asked, "Who is it?"

"Sayaka."

Opening the door, The Golden Amazon stepped back. She made no move to either hide her nudity or the fact that she held her sword.

If the onna-bugeisha was concerned by either, she didn't show it. Her face remained as expressionless as always. "May I enter?"

"Feel free." The Golden Amazon had not spent any private time with her new teammates, instead focusing on remaining alone so she could pursue her own interests... but she knew that Bushido and Nemesis had been going out of their way to pay attention to Eidolon so she was not entirely surprised to have one of them drop in on her. "What do you want?" she asked, not eager to indulge in frivolous conversation. These people were not her friends and certainly not her equals.

"We will have to watch Eidolon."

"What do you mean?" she asked, shutting the door behind the Japanese warrior.

"I eavesdropped on a conversation he had with Nemesis - he shot Eun Jiwon and left him for dead, but he could have killed him. Now, we have no way of knowing whether or not Assistance Unlimited saved him."

"You'll know eventually," the Amazon replied. Sighing, she added, "I already made it clear that I don't trust him. He's a spy."

"That I don't know... but I do know that Nemesis believes he is useful and isn't willing to discard him, no matter how much I think it would be wise to do so."

"You share the man's bed... can't you convince him to do whatever you want? Men don't always think with their head. That's yet another reason why women make better leaders."

Bushido actually allowed a quick smile to disturb the expressionless mask of her face. "Nemesis is not like most men. His spirit can't be broken by sex."

"Not by *your* sex, perhaps."

Bushido's smile turned into a grimace. "Are you suggesting that you could do better than I have?"

"It is not a suggestion. I am as skilled in the arts of lovemaking as I am in battle. If I chose to, I could not only bend him to my will - I could such pleasures that he would die from the intensity of them."

The two women stared at one another for a silent moment that seemed to stretch into eternity. They were once more sizing each other up, though this time there was a different quality to it. No longer were they taking measure of each other for combat... but for a different sort of struggle.

"I believe you," Bushido said at last. She reached out and placed a hand on The Golden Amazon's hip. "Would you be willing to teach me? I would like to exert a greater control over him."

"You would never be my equal. I have been chemically altered so that I am capable of more than any other woman." Despite her words, she pulled Bushido to her. The onna-bugeisha felt the heat as the larger woman's breasts flattened against her. "I can give you tips, however. As with all things, it is best to instruct by showing rather than by describing."

Bushido allowed the Amazon to take the lead - she tilted her head back and felt the other woman's tongue push past her parted lips.

Outside, the city seethed like an animal.

CHAPTER X
TO FACE THE MAD GOD!

DAWN BROKE OVER Sovereign City, but it did not bring sunlight and warmth. A storm moved in just before the morning commute to work began and heavy rainfall began to drench the city streets. Sovereign was known for its rainy weather and its residents had a tendency to treat every day with the expectation that it would require a raincoat or an umbrella.

Abby Cross didn't think she'd ever get used to the foul weather. Having grown up in Louisiana, she'd become accustomed to sunny skies, hot summers and the occasional drought.

She stood in front of a large window in the team's meeting room, watching as the skies released their pent-up aggression upon the city. She hadn't slept well... she'd had a dream about Jakob. Her former lover had returned to Robeson Avenue, but it wasn't to make up with her or with Lazarus... he'd come with pistol in hand, saying that he'd come to end them all. He'd shot Lazarus first, then turned the gun on one member of the team after another... until all that was left was Abby. During the conflict, she'd been unable to call upon her magic for some reason... she'd stood mute and helpless as Jakob had dispatched them all. When they'd finally faced each other over the bodies of their friends, she'd felt torn between her feelings for him and horror over what he had done.

And then he'd killed her, too.

Premonitions weren't her stock-in-trade, but she knew better than to completely ignore a vivid dream.

"Abby?"

She jerked with a start, realizing that Lazarus was standing beside her. He had managed to enter the room without her even noticing. With a sheepish grin, she said, "I'm sorry. I was lost in thought."

"Anything you need to talk about?"

"No, not really."

Lazarus nodded and took a seat at the large table that dominated the room. "Does it have to do with Jakob?"

Abby's eyes widened. "Why would you--?"

"You were very close to him, but you hardly ever mention him. It was just an assumption."

"Well, you're not wrong. I had a dream about him... but it wasn't a pleasant one. In my dream, he came here and shot all of us."

Without hesitation, Lazarus replied, "He shot Eun."

"What? Are you sure?"

"Dr. Hancock fished out the bullets this morning - it came from a 1910 Mauser and Jakob uses one. Plus, the shots came very close to killing him... perhaps it was mere chance or divine providence that saved Eun's life, but I think it may have been a skilled marksman. Again, Jakob fits that description. Finally, we have the fact that someone called in the shooting... I'd like to think that Jakob, if he had done this, wouldn't allow Eun to just bleed out. I think he shot Eun, made sure that none of the bullets would prove fatal and called us to ensure that he was found before it was too late."

"But... why?"

"If he was at Holder Way, he might be investigating Murder Unlimited on his own and Eun got in his way... or he might be working with Murder Unlimited."

"You can't believe that. Jakob wouldn't do that. He might have had a philosophical difference of opinion, but he was still our friend. I might -- might -- be able to envision a scenario where he would have had to shoot Eun, but I refuse to believe that he's turned completely against us."

"I hope you're right," Lazarus said, and Abby could tell that he meant it. "Now, are you ready for what we talked about?"

Abby nodded, grateful for the change in subject. She took a seat across from Lazarus and placed her palms flat on the tabletop. "I spent a little time with Sally before coming here -- well, I guess I should call her Thrúd, shouldn't I? Anyway, I used a spell to help me recognize the Asgardian energy that permeates her clothing and hammer. Using that, I think I'll be able to home in on any site in the city that contains a sizeable amount of the energy."

"Which should, in theory, lead us to Murder Unlimited," Lazarus said.

"That's the idea, anyway," Abby replied. "Want me to get started?"

Lazarus nodded and fell silent, not wanting to distract her. The way her magic worked was still a mystery to him… he'd taken part in rituals that dealt with supernatural forces, but he lacked whatever gift Abby possessed that allowed her to directly channel magical energy through her own body.

Abby closed her eyes and began moving her lips, reciting a spell that had been written in the Dark Ages by a monk named Mathias that sought to locate the stolen bones of a saint. It had proven successful in his search and since then it had become popular with witches and wizards that needed a searching spell that didn't go over into black magic.

She felt a stirring in her brain, one that spread out until it encompassed her entire upper body. Her lips parted and a shudder ran through her shoulders. She could sense that Asgardian energy out there in the city and she cast out an astral version of her body in search of it. Invisible to the naked eye, this astral body traveled through Sovereign, led like a bloodhound by the power of the spell. She was drawn to a pleasant-looking building on the west side of town and she passed right through the walls, where she saw several things that concerned her -- first she saw a room filled with scavenged items from Asgard. There were weapons, books and clothing, as well as things that she couldn't begin to guess as to their purpose. Next, she saw various people that apparently lived in this building… and all of them she recognized: Nemesis, Bushido, The Golden Amazon… and Eidolon. While the notion that The Golden Amazon would ally herself with Murder Unlimited was surprising, it was the presence of Jakob that broke her heart.

Lazarus had been right.

She saw her former lover working out with Bushido, practicing some form of martial arts under her tutelage. He was obviously no prisoner… he was one of them.

Realizing that she had valuable information - confirmation of who made up Murder Unlimited and the address of their abode - - she started to pull away from the location, intending to send her astral body back to her physical form.

She found her way back blocked by some sort of mystical barrier and no matter how hard she tried to break free, she was unable to return to her body. With a cry of alarm, she felt a psychic tendril wrap around her astral body, pulling her towards some unknown place.

Abby saw the city below her become a blur and her surroundings didn't settle into something that she could understand until it was too late. She was on her knees, bound by some sort of psychic bonds... and she found herself in front of a man with long reddish-blond hair and a thick beard. He wore a fur cloak slung over one shoulder but was otherwise bare-chested. He wore leather pants and furred boots that were wrapped about his legs. He sat in a large wooden chair; an antique thing that looked like something Abby could have found in one of the higher-priced antique shops. There was no way to describe it as anything besides a throne.

Whoever he was, he was a powerful mage... taking an astral body prisoner was no small feat. It was also a dangerous thing - at least for Abby. If a spirit was kept from its physical form for too long, they could become trapped on the astral plane. How long that took varied from person to person and was influenced by their force of will, their age and even their physical health.

"Who are you?" Abby asked.

The bearded man leaned forward and chuckled. "Hello, fair one. I am Loki."

LAZARUS KNEW THAT something was wrong, but he had no way of identifying what it was.

Minutes had passed since Abby had begun her spell... and though Lazarus didn't know the ins and outs of this particular ritual, he was beginning to feel that she should have returned by now. Had she somehow been discovered by a member of Murder Unlimited? It wasn't out of the realm of possibility that

Nemesis might have sought out a witch of his own -- he did seem obsessed with duplicating Lazarus at times.

The meeting room door opened, and Lazarus glanced over to see Thrúd enter. The daughter of Thor was not wearing her helmet and Lazarus was intrigued to notice how similar - and yet different - her features were from Sally Weatherby's. They were slightly more angular now; the softness having been replaced by a firm setting of the jaw and a toughening of the eyes. He noticed that her hammer was slipped through her belt, the bashing side hanging down against her hip. "Am I interrupting?" she asked, looking from Lazarus to Abby and back again.

"Not at all - in fact, you might be the only person that could help." Lazarus stood up and moved around to stand next to Abby. The young woman was sitting ramrod straight, eyes closed. Her breathing was rapid and growing more so. "Abby cast a spell to try and locate the missing Asgardian items but I'm growing concerned about her. Do you think you could help somehow?"

Thrúd needed no further encouragement. She came forward quickly and knelt at Abby's side, reaching out to firmly grip one of the woman's wrists. "I am no magician, friend Lazarus, but I am more attuned to the supernatural than most mortals. You are wise to fear for her... I can sense that her soul is held by another. Further, the scent of fair Asgard is radiating off of her!"

"What does that mean? Is someone using an Asgardian object to bind her?"

"Worse than that, I fear -- someone with potent Asgardian *power* is doing this directly."

"A sorcerer?"

"Someone with this level of ability is beyond a mere sorcerer," Thrúd said. "Only a true god would have the power to trap someone like Abby."

"Can you free her?"

"I can try," Thrúd said but her words didn't imply much faith in her ability to carry it through. "I fear that my uncle is behind this."

Lazarus simply nodded. He had already guessed as much - Durok had made it clear that he served Loki and Thrúd had implicated her uncle in the destruction of Asgard, so it made sense to see Loki as the biggest threat here. The question now was: had Loki somehow seized Abby from her reconnaissance mission or was Loki actually working with Murder Unlimited? If so, it was once again a case of Lazarus and Nemesis dancing around one another in perfect step: were they both allied with a god now - one with Thrúd and the other with Loki?

Thrúd kept one hand on Abby's wrist and the other she put on the back of the brunette's head. The physical connection allowed her to share some of her divine energy with Abby -- it was like providing an extra boost of strength to someone that was struggling to lift a heavy weight.

"I don't know if this will be enough to allow her to escape," Thrúd admitted. "I can only hope that she's able to tap into my power and use it to do what she must."

———— ∞∞∞ ————

LOKI STOOD UP from his throne and approached Abby, seemingly enjoying the way she struggled against her psychic bonds. "You are an enticing little creature," he said. "In the past, I've always considered mortal women to be like cream puffs - tasty but insubstantial. You seem to be formed of sterner stuff."

"Release me and I'll show you how strong I really am."

"I think not." Moving behind her, Loki let his fingers trail through her hair. She shuddered involuntarily and her face darkened with rising anger. She prided herself on her inner strength and to be held prisoner like this set her on edge. "What were you doing on the astral plane, my sweet?"

"Go to hell."

"I've been there. Its ruler is a relative of mine." Loki let his fingers become entangled in her hair and he gripped it, pulling against her scalp until her head was jerked back. Even though this astral body was not her true form, attacks of magical or psychic natures could result in harm in the real world. "Now, again, tell me what you're up to…"

Realizing that resisting would only prolong her time away from her body, Abby said, "I was investigating the theft of Asgardian artifacts by a group known as Murder Unlimited. I found them but before I could make it back to tell my friends, you snared me!"

Loki released her and began stroking his beard, tugging at it thoughtfully. "Your friends... Assistance Unlimited. Lazarus Gray. Durok has told me of them. I believe my niece is staying at their headquarters."

"If she finds you, she's going to use that hammer of hers to bust your head open," Abby taunted.

"I'm sure she'd like to try," Loki said. "Like her idiot father, she's not capable of realizing when she's outclassed." He stepped in front of her and knelt, bringing his eyes level with hers. "Now, this Murder Unlimited you mentioned... tell me more."

"A handful of criminals," she muttered, not wanting to add that her former lover was one of them. "Nobody important."

"I know enough of Lazarus to know that he's dangerous... so perhaps it would make sense for me to have my own team to combat his own. That would free me up to destroy this world and stand at the breach to help guide the birth of the next."

Abby felt a sudden surge of strength and she realized that the bonds that held her fast were no longer as imposing as before. In fact, she was certain that if she applied enough pressure to them, she could free herself...

Abby wondered where this newfound energy was coming from, but she was definitely not going to look a proverbial gift horse in the mouth. Still, she wanted to be careful lest Loki see that she was now a threat to escape and bring his power to bear against her.

"You know," she said, disdain dripping with every word, "I've met a handful of you so-called 'gods' and I've noticed something: you're no better than us 'mere mortals.' You're just as petty as we are... maybe more so. The only difference is you guys are longer lived."

"And we're more powerful," he said warningly. "You forgot that."

Abby hid her smile. She could hear his anger in his reply, and she knew that he was annoyed by her words. While he turned away from her, hands clenched into fists, she was able to make her move. She flexed her arms, using the added power she'd somehow picked up to break the psychic bonds that Loki had cast around her.

Loki seemed to sense that something had happened because he whirled about, and his eyes grew wide as he saw Abby launching herself at him. She delivered a roundhouse punch that rocked him on his heels -- it was a psychic blow rather than a physical one, but it was more than enough to send Loki reeling.

As the god of mischief shook his head to clear it, Abby caught him with a backhanded blow that knocked him into his throne and sent the chair toppling over.

"I'm going to leave you now," Abby said, hoping that she sounded more confident than she actually felt. Even with this newfound power, she was severely outclassed - if Loki struck quickly enough, he could skewer her and kill both her astral and physical selves. "But if I ever see you again, I'm not going to stop until I've beaten you to a pulp!"

Without waiting for Loki to respond, Abby brought both fists up in front of her face and then slammed her arms together. This gesture was the final part of the spell and signaled that it was time for her astral body to return to its physical shell.

She vanished from Loki's sight and her body suddenly jerked forward in the meeting room. She sucked in air like she'd been drowning, and she looked around with wide eyes at both Lazarus and Thrúd. "Loki," she gasped. "Loki!"

Lazarus frowned and started to move away, intending to summon the rest of the group -- he was stopped when Abby seized him by the arm. "There's more?"

Abby glanced away, not able to meet his gaze. "I found Murder Unlimited."

"You saw Jakob," he said. It wasn't a question because he could see the truth of it in her expression.

"Not just him. The Golden Amazon is with them, too." Shakily, she rose to her feet and the momentary vulnerability that he'd seen in her features vanished suddenly. She was once more the self-confident woman that he had come to reply upon so heavily. "We need to strike fast, Lazarus... before they have a chance to prepare for us."

Thrúd pulled her hammer from its place on her belt. "The daughter of Thor shall fight at your side, my friends!"

Lazarus gave a nod of thanks but inside he wondered if

that would be enough... Nemesis and Bushido were dangerous enough but if Eidolon and The Golden Amazon had joined them, they had the power and knowledge to lay Assistance Unlimited low.

And then, of course, there was Loki.

———❦———

THE GOD OF Mischief was seething with anger. The girl had played him somehow, tapping into his emotions and using them to cause him to overlook her actions.

Still, something good had come of the exchange... he had learned of Murder Unlimited. He cast a withering look at Durok as the man came forward to check on him and his loyal follower shrank away in fear that his master was about to strike and replace him with another version of himself.

Without a word to Durok, Loki left the apartment that had once belonged to his human host. He had plucked the address of Murder Unlimited's lair from the mortal woman's brain and he cursed himself for not having looked further while he'd been there - perhaps he could have seen what she was up to.

No matter, he would allow his enemies this small victory... in the end, it would not matter at all.

———❦———

LESS THAN TEN minutes later, Paul Alfred Müller-Murnau was stepping from the shower when he realized that he was not alone. A strange, bearded man was in the bathroom with him, barely visible through the steam that hung in the air.

Nemesis reacted without hesitation, snatching up a towel from a nearby hanger and whipping it at the stranger. The bearded man merely smiled and seized hold of the cloth as it whipped by his face. He yanked on it, pulling Nemesis across the slick floor.

Nemesis released his hold on the towel but was unable to stop himself from skidding towards the intruder. He readied himself for an attack, but the man merely caught Nemesis around the waist and helped him stabilize himself.

"Let's not play games," the stranger said. "You're not going to harm me with a towel, I can promise you."

"Who are you?" Nemesis asked, taking a step back and regarding the man with suspicion. He could tell this figure was powerful -- he practically radiated confidence and there was a mystical aura that surrounded him. He pondered why that aura seemed familiar - and then it suddenly came to him: this person felt just like the Asgardian artifacts that he'd been studying. "You're from Asgard," he said before Loki had a chance to answer.

"Yes, I am... I'm one of the few survivors of the Golden Realm." Loki smiled cruelly. "In fact, I'm one of the architects of its demise."

"Loki," Nemesis whispered, his eyes growing wide. He forgot his nakedness and instead dropped to one knee, supplicating himself before one of the ancient beings that he had once idolized as a boy. "I am a faithful Aryan, my lord, and willing to serve you as you see fit."

Loki stared at him and then chuckled. "Rise, my pet. You are a faithful cur, aren't you? I do admire mortals that recognize their place."

What happened next was the most shocking moment in Loki's long existence - for the second time within a half hour, a mortal did not behave as he'd expected... and this time it would prove to be a fatal mistake on the god's part.

Nemesis launched himself upward, wrapping his strong hands on either side of Loki's head. He gave a tremendous twist and the neck that had once belonged to Mike Simms was snapped with a crack that seemed unnaturally loud in the bathroom.

Prepared for what he knew would come next, Müller-Murnau quickly uttered a series of phrases that were spoken in the language of the ancient Atlanteans, whom he knew to be Aryans lost to the world in the ancient past. He'd made a study of such things and since joining forces with the OFP, he'd been able to gain access to ancient tomes that had further solidified his wisdom on the subject.

Even as Loki's spirit was cast out of the now dead human shell it had been occupying, it was drawn straight into Müller-Murnau's. Nemesis cast the corpse aside and took a deep breath, willing himself to start a mental combat with the God of Mischief.

Loki immediately set about trying to seize control of the man's body but Müller-Murnau was far different than any mortal that the Asgardian had attempted to inhabit before. This man was the spiritual mirror image of Lazarus Gray, who had battled his way through hell and back. Müller-Murnau continued to whisper his Atlantean phrases even as his body began to convulse from the tremendous struggle going on inside of him.

He had read in one of the Asgardian scrolls that his people had brought him of the gods' methods of inhabiting mortal bodies. Such things could allow the gods to survive the destruction of their godly forms but it came with a price - they could be killed as any other mortal could be, though a powerful sorcerer like Loki could simply move his soul into yet another host... but Nemesis was confident that he could reverse the usual result. Instead of having his own mind locked away in a prison, he sought to do the same to Loki. If he succeeded, he would have Loki's power, but it would be Müller-Murnau that controlled it.

Though no one else in the city knew it, a battle of epic proportions was taking place, with ramifications that would reverberate around the world.

—❧—

BUSHIDO FROWNED, LOOKING up at the clock that hung on the wall of her room. She'd heard Nemesis go to take his shower and then had heard the water turned off when he'd finished... but minutes had passed since then, and she hadn't heard him leave the bathroom. No matter what personal matters he might be attending to, it was becoming excessive how long he was taking. Perhaps, she mused, he had slipped and fallen? If so, he might need assistance.

Rising from her bed, she exited her room and paused outside the bathroom door. She was about to knock when it opened to reveal Nemesis. He wore only a towel wrapped about his waist, his flawless physique glistening from the shower.

"Paul?" she asked, concerned by the way he seemed to be almost *glowing*. She was intimately familiar with every aspect of his body and this was different, somehow.

Waving the fingers of his right hand through the air, he

telekinetically pulled Bushido against him. He kissed her - hard - and when he pulled away, she was breathless and staring at him. "No longer will I live in Lazarus Gray's shadow," he said, his voice carrying more strength than she'd heard in it before. "I will be the sun that burns him to a crisp."

CHAPTER XI
THE WIDENING THREAT

"**D**AMN IT."

Morgan glanced over at Lazarus, surprised by what amounted to a tremendous outburst of frustration for his friend and leader. Lazarus was known for being mostly emotionless in the field - indeed, many people that didn't know him well thought him almost robotic in his interactions with others. To have him verbally display his anger, even if it was muttered half under his breath, was quite unusual.

Assistance Unlimited had come en masse to the location found by Abby but they'd found the place scrubbed clean of any sign of the villains. All of Murder Unlimited's clothing, weapons, food and more were gone... indeed, the place looked like no one had lived here in months, if not years.

"How is this possible?" Lazarus asked, looking around at the rest of the team. They were standing in a large open room that Morgan figured must have either been a meeting area or an exercise floor. "It took us less than half an hour to get here." Looking at Abby, he asked, "Are you certain that what you saw was in the present and not the past?"

"Positive."

"Again -- how is this possible?" Lazarus wondered aloud.

"My uncle was here," Thrúd said and all eyes immediately turned upon her. Her lower face was exposed beneath her helm and her mouth was twisted in disgust, as if she alone could smell something foul. "His stench permeates this place. If he wished, he could have spirited them away."

"I could always try to locate them again," Abby offered. "With Thrúd around to help me, maybe I could even avoid Loki."

"Too dangerous," Lazarus replied with a shake of his head.

"We nearly lost you last time."

"We're not alone," Kelly said. She had been standing near the stairs that led to the floors below and now she was backing away from them, her body dropping into a fighting stance.

Morgan heard it now, too -- the heavy footfalls of many feet, some of them booted. What sounded like a small army was rushing up the stairs and Morgan drew his pistol, realizing that not only had their enemies had time to flee but that they'd left behind an ambush, as well.

A roar of voices joined in with the thunder of approaching feet, shouting expletives and promises of pain. Some of their words were unfamiliar to the heroes of Assistance Unlimited, sounding like they were in an ancient tongue.

Lazarus shouted, "Defensive pattern alpha!" and the members of Assistance Unlimited fell into their assigned positions: The Black Terror was positioned at the front of an arrow-shaped formation, with Kelly, Lazarus and Samantha arranged to his left; to the right were Thrúd, Abby and Morgan.

Anyone that came up the stairs would be first confronted with the superpowered fury of The Black Terror - if the group made it past him, their ranks would be split down the middle, allowing the rest of the team to take them on. Thrúd was occupying the slot that normally would have been given over to Eun and she was eager to test her mettle in combat.

The horde that burst into the room was comprised of Viking warriors, armed with axes and spears, and white jumpsuited agents of Murder Unlimited brandishing pistols.

The first of the invaders was confronted by The Black Terror - he grabbed a Viking by the beard and hurled him back into the crowd, knocking several back down the stairs.

Another swung a heavy axe at Bob and the hero blocked it with a forearm, letting the steel shatter against his skin. With a roar that matched those of his enemies, The Black Terror lowered a shoulder and ran right into the middle of the army with all the force of a fullback, knocking many of them aside.

Thrúd struck next, spinning her hammer before swinging it like a big-league slugger. She caught one of the Murder Unlimited stooges in the chest, shattering multiple ribs and taking him out of the fight in one hit. If she hadn't pulled her blow, she would have removed him from the mortal plane, as well.

Bullets began to fly, most of them from the villainous horde but some of Assistance Unlimited responded in kind: Morgan and Samantha both opened fire on their enemies, using their pinpoint accuracy to remove the ones they decided posed the greatest threat.

Lazarus and his wife proved to be an effective pair, falling into place back to back and using a symbiotic fighting style that maximized their respective strengths. Lazarus was a trained fighter that focused on well-delivered punches to key spots on his enemies' bodies while Kelly was nimble enough to utilize her speed and grace to avoid blows from her Viking foes while delivering pulverizing kicks from her strong legs.

Abby focused most of her abilities on protecting her friends. She cast a glamor that made them all appear to be several feet away from their actual positions, reducing the chances of them getting shot. When one of the Murder Unlimited soldiers came to close, she did manage to sneak in an open-handed palm strike to his throat and then followed up with an elbow that shattered the man's nose.

Despite the fact that they were outnumbered nearly four to one, the battle was rather brief and one-sided. Assistance Unlimited ended up standing in the midst of their beaten foes, many of whom groaned in pain while others were blissfully unconscious.

Kelly let out a gasp as the Vikings began fading away, seemingly evaporating. The process seemed painful as their moanings intensified... in the aftermath, all that was left were the footsoldiers of Murder Unlimited.

Lazarus seized one of the nearest men by the hair on the back of his head, pulling him up to his knees and staring into the man's bloodied face. A bullet was lodged in the fellow's shoulder and he was missing two front teeth. "What's your name?" Lazarus asked, tightening his grip when the fellow hesitated.

"Maxwell," the man finally gasped out, wincing in pain.

"Listen closely, Maxwell... your only hope of getting us to put in a good word for you with the authorities is to answer all of my questions. Understand?"

Maxwell grinned and spat out a mixture of phlegm and

blood. The disgusting mass landed on the front of Lazarus' shirt and began to ooze its way down. "The judges here are in my bosses' back pockets. They'll have me back on the streets within an hour!"

"Not if I throw you straight into Tartarus," Lazarus warned, bringing up the super-prison that he housed his worst foes. "I was given the okay to hold dangerous villains there without having to go through the courts -- I'm sure you've heard about it, haven't you?"

Maxwell grimaced as he swallowed a mouthful of blood. "That place isn't meant for guys like me," he stammered.

"He's right," Morgan said, coming to stand near Lazarus. "You throw this loser in there and those other prisoners will rip him to shreds within a day!"

Maxwell looked nervously from Lazarus to Morgan, not picking up on the bit of play-acting that was taking place.

Lazarus looked contemplative and then shook his head. "If they kill him, it'll be his own fault. He's right - we can't turn him over to the police so whatever happens, happens."

"Wait!" Maxwell exclaimed. "I'll talk, I'll talk! Just... tell me what you want to know."

"Where is Nemesis?"

Maxwell sighed and said, "You won't believe it."

"Try me."

"He told me that they were going to the last outpost of Atlantis... a place called Vorium."

SIX HOURS LATER

THE ICY WIND whipped through the open window of the military-style truck, biting into Müller-Murnau's cheeks, turning them a bright red. Seated beside him was Bushido, heavily bundled. Both of them were rocked back and forth as he drove the vehicle over the ice. He was being careful not to lose control of the truck in these slick conditions.

He braked before a massive upright chunk of ice. The

wooden black hull of a 19th-century sailing ship could be seen underneath the thick layers of ice. Caught in an ice floe many years ago, the vessel was a wreck of a ship, one that had refused to die at sea. Here on the Mer de Glace, it had become a forgotten relic of a bygone era.

"Tell me again why we're here," Bushido asked. She had not touched him since their unexpected kiss... he was different now, infused with the essence of a being that she did not care for. Nemesis had dominated the mind of Loki but there was a still certain amount of bleed-over that made her uncomfortable.

"You know of my long-time fascination with Atlantis. I believed that the brilliant men and women that lived there were my Aryan ancestors. This desolate land is home to the final outpost of that paradise. Vorium was founded by survivors from the lost continent of Atlantis. Their scientific and mystical knowledge far surpasses anything we possess in the outside world."

He turned off the truck's engine and exited the cab, Bushido following suit. "We have the Asgardian weaponry... why do we need anything from Vorium? We can go ahead and kill Lazarus now." she said.

Nemesis sighed, pulling his fur-lined collar closer to his neck. "I've decided that getting rid of Lazarus can wait. We have enough firepower to obliterate him and all his agents... so why not focus on bigger game for now?"

"That wasn't our agreement," Eidolon said. The masked figure was in the process of dropping out of the back of the truck. "I'm sure The Golden Amazon would agree with me that we're not working with you to find Atlantis or to stoke your Aryan ego... we want to take down Assistance Unlimited."

The statuesque Amazon clambered out and looked around at their snowy environment with obvious disdain. "He's right... when you told us we had to flee our home; I was worried that you were becoming a coward. Now I realize that you are just revealing your true colors: you care nothing for my mission or even for destroying your enemy. All you want is to seize more power for yourself."

Nemesis turned to face his mutinous allies and one corner of his mouth turned upward in a smile. When he spoke, his voice was full of mirth... and madness. "I *have* power, Jakob... or are you forgetting how I was able to teleport our clothes, our weapons and all of our other belongings out of or apartment building? I have the power of Loki! Despite the fact that I can feel him fighting against me, I have bested him! Be patient, my friends - and I will give you all that I have promised... and more! Eidolon, I will personally slay all those you have deemed worthy of death. Evil shall quake at your name - and at mine! As for you, my lovely Amazon... I will give you dominion over half the earth! When you have solidified your power there, we will discuss what to do with the other half."

"And me?" Bushido asked. She had subtly moved away from him, her hand coming to rest on the hilt of her long, curved blade.

"You will be the mother of Loki's child," he said, turning his gaze upon her. What more could you ask for?"

"I wished to be the mother of *your* child."

"It's the same thing."

Silence fell over the wintry plateau and Nemesis broke the peace by turning back towards the mountain of ice and snow. "There is a cave nearby... it will lead us into the earth. From what I have read, we will find a side passage after a long trek... we should take it. After another mile or so, we will notice a light beginning to illuminate our path. That will be the artificial sun that warms the inner world of Vorium." He began walking and his words drifted back to them over his shoulder. "Turn back now if you wish but I am pressing on. Your choice should be a simple one: serve at the hand of god or go back to your lives of disappointment and despair."

The other three members of the team paused, and Bushido realized that Eidolon and The Golden Amazon were staring at her, as if waiting for her to make the decision for them.

After a moment in which she ran through various scenarios in her head, Bushido said, "We should follow him... for now. If it looks like he has lost himself to Loki and is planning to betray him, we owe it to the man he was to slay the beast he has become."

THEY MOVED DOWN the icy passage, noting that the temperature was slowly rising as they did so. They had been walking down into the bowels of the Earth for what seemed an eternity, the eyes of Eidolon and Bushido unable to pierce the gloom. It fell to Nemesis and The Golden Amazon to lead the way - Nemesis seemed unaffected by the darkness while The Amazon's vision was acute enough to make out the basic path that they were following.

Gradually, the passage became clearer and Nemesis could not only spot a light in the distance but the scent of vegetation and heady perfumes. He moved faster; his gloved hands kept close to the pouches that lined the interior of his fur-lined coat. Inside them were a wide variety of powders, weapons, and mystic artifacts - some of them of Asgardian origin. He had brought along everything he thought might prove useful... after all, Loki might find a way to prevent him from utilizing his powers and he didn't want to be caught wanting at a key moment.

Nemesis emerged from the cave, blinking in the artificial sunlight. They were atop a cliff overlooking the city. He looked up to see that Vorium was located beneath a huge rocky dome, from which hung a mechanized "sun."

Down below, towering spires and densely packed streets could be seen, with hundreds of men and women walking amongst them. The men wore loose-fitting clothing, mostly in blues, whites, and grays, while the women were dressed in tight blouses and short skirts that revealed far more leg than would be acceptable in polite society.

But it was the creature that suddenly soared past them that most surprised Nemesis, for as its leathery wings beat wildly, propelling it higher into the sky.

Eidolon gasped, recognizing it for what it was immediately: a pterodactyl. "That's impossible," he whispered.

Scanning the city once more, Nemesis spotted several more prehistoric creatures being used as beasts of burden by the Voriums. This interior world was not home to a lost race of people - it was the final resting place for creatures long thought extinct!

"We've been spotted," The Golden Amazon warned. She

drew her sword and stepped in front of the others, presenting herself before the new arrivals: a small congregation of men and women that were approaching on a path that led up from the city.

Nemesis warned her, "Don't attack them unless they make a move towards us. I don't want these people to view us as the enemy."

"I know how to do my job," she replied, bristling at the way he continued to bark out orders to her. She wasn't sure how long she could continue putting up with him. Now that he had Loki's power, he was even more insufferable.

"Welcome," said the man at the front of the Vorium party. He looked like he was in his late fifties, with white hair, thick eyebrows and a slender frame. "I am Lex, the current Superintendent of the city."

"You don't seem very surprised to see us," The Golden Amazon said, relaxing her stance slightly. She didn't sheath her blade, but she did lower it. For his part, Lex seemed to take no notice of her weapon.

"That's because we're not," Lex replied. "Our people see science and magic as intertwined… there is little difference between the two. Just as we have mastered the technology required to power our sun and run our electromagnetic generators, we have trained some of our people to read the signs of prophecy. We were told that a group would come, bearing three members of pure Aryan blood… and one mongrel."

Eidolon looked quickly at Bushido, realizing for whom that slur was aimed. As a former member of the Schutzstaffel, Jakob knew that his ancestry was pure - and given The Golden Amazon's flawless appearance, she as the very epitome of the Aryan ideal. Nemesis was much the same - even more so now that he was sharing his body with a Nordic god.

That left poor Bushido as the only member of their group that lacked the 'proper' genetics.

Jakob had always considered much of the 'racial purity' talk to be nonsense but he wasn't surprised that Lex and his people would hold fast to such beliefs. Still, he tensed, expecting Nemesis to respond with anger - Bushido had told Jakob that not too long ago, an agent of the OFP had referred to her in similar terms and that Nemesis had gone out of his way to not only refute them but to deliver physical harm to the man.

To his surprise - and, evidently, to Bushido's, Müller-Murnau responded quite differently this time. Murder Unlimited's leader simply said, "Your soothsayers were correct, then... and did they tell you that one of us would not only be the perfect Aryan Übermensch but also the bearer of a godly power?"

Lex gave a shake of his head. "No, they did not... and this Übermensch is you, I presume?"

"It is. The power of Loki flows through my veins."

"Impressive," Lex replied in such a placid tone that Jakob wondered if the man simply didn't believe it at all. "We have kept up with the outside world and know of that war that threatens to consume it. As such, we have taken safeguards to ensure that our paradise can never be destroyed by the machinations of Presidents, Prime Ministers or even Fuehrers."

The Golden Amazon found that intriguing enough to speak up. She asked, "What precautions have you taken?"

Jakob knew she was probably less concerned with the impact their plans could have on current world leaders than she was with whether or not they could potentially impact her own schemes for world domination.

"We have planted machines in key locations that can warm the polar ice caps, causing them to melt at such a rate that the world's oceans will rise to a dangerous level, flooding much of civilization. We'll be perfectly safe here, but a majority of the world will be killed within days." Lex spoke with undeniable pride at these words. "But that's hardly the reason why you came to see us, is it? You're here to restore your connection to your Aryan roots."

Nemesis nodded and said, "I'm afraid that we'll probably be bringing more visitors your way. We have enemies that will try and follow us here -- and given how capable they are, I have no doubt that they'll find the entrance to Vorium."

"Then I'll assign a few men to guard the entrance -- whomever your enemies are, they'll be taken aback by the welcome we'll give them." Lex reached out and clasped Nemesis on the forearm and said, "This is our traditional way of accepting newcomers to our ranks."

"Thank you," Nemesis said, and he genuinely meant it. After a lifetime of believing in the stories of Aryan superiority, it was wonderful to see physical proof that they had all been real.

Turning to the others in his party, Lex clapped his hands together three times. The men and women, all of whom were uniformly attractive, moved to take Nemesis, Eidolon and The Golden Amazon by the arms. They cooed and stroked the trio, promising to show them every part of Vorium.

Bushido watched as her companions were led down the path into the city. Only she and Lex remained on the cliff's edge, staring at each other with undisguised distaste.

"We have a few non-Aryans here," the older man said. "You would be welcome to join them in serving us... given your physicality, I would think you would make a welcome addition to the ranks of comfort women."

Bushido struck with the quickness of a cobra. Her blade sliced through the air would have decapitated Lex had the Vorium leader not displayed his own incredible skill. He caught the blade with one palm on each side of the weapon, smiling at the look of amazement on Bushido's face. He then lifted one foot and drove it hard into her midsection, sending her tumbling back and causing her to lose her grip on the blade's handle.

The Japanese woman rolled back to her feet with impressive speed, one hand falling protectively over her stomach. She felt the baby kick inside her, but she worried that the blow might have hurt her unborn child. With the rage of a mother, she hissed, "Touch me one more time and I will cut out your intestines and choke you with them."

"Strong words but forgive me if I doubt your ability to follow through on them." Lex tossed her weapon at her feet and turned away from her. "Follow me if you like... but do please remember that you are not of our people, despite the child you carry in your belly."

"How do you--?"

"I'm perceptive enough to notice your pregnancy and wise enough to know that the only reason those two Aryans would keep you about is if you were spreading your legs for one of them. Or both."

Bushido snatched up her blade and considered making

another attempt at ending the smug bastard's life but she held off, knowing that somehow he would only stop her... the locals were obviously not just brilliant and good-looking, they were skilled combatants as well. She would bide her time.

———— ∞ ————

LAZARUS GRAY PILOTED the team's private plane with practiced skill. They were nearing the site of Vorium's supposed location, a site that was known to only a few -- and believed by even less. The copilot's seat was occupied by Samantha while the rest of the team that had accompanied them -- Thrúd, Morgan and The Black Terror -- were in the rear of the plane. Eun was still hospitalized and Kelly had remained behind to watch over the kids, meaning that the team was not at full strength... but the addition of Thor's daughter would hopefully compensate for that.

It had taken precious time for Lazarus to research Vorium... thankfully, his library was second to none in North America. Someday, he mused, he'd like to be able to build a massive card catalog of his holdings, cross-referenced by author, subject and title. Until then, he had to manually look through the books until he eventually found what he was looking for. In this case, a detailed history of Vorium was located in a small chapter of *Ancient Aryan Races* by Prof. A.L. Garcia. It didn't provide many details, but it did claim that an offshoot of Atlantis had somehow found a way into the earth's interior, colonizing it with the help of their advanced science.

Thrúd had sped them along when she'd insistently stated that her uncle's spirit was now housed with the body of Nemesis. She said that this knowledge had come to her via a raven that had perched on her shoulder and whispered this dark fact in her ear. She said this bird had been one of grandfather's pet ravens - Huginn, to be precise, and that he had fallen to dust shortly after.

Lazarus noted that Samantha had been very quiet during their flight and he cleared his throat before asking, "How are you holding up?"

"I'm fine."

"Cord was a good man. We're all going to miss him."

Samantha paused before looking out the window. "You'll miss having a police officer that's on our side... but he was a little more than that to me. I was as surprised as anyone when we hit it off but there were sides to him that nobody else got to see. I just wish it had ended better for us."

"He should have trusted you," Lazarus said. "I understand why he didn't believe you when you said your pregnancy wasn't from an affair but given the strangeness he'd seen with his own eyes, I think he should have given you the benefit of the doubt."

"Well, he didn't. Now I'm an unwed mother, my father is scandalized and Cord's dead." She reached up and began pulling her hair back into a ponytail, tying it with a band. Like the rest of the team, she was outfitted for the icy conditions in which they would be landing. "I appreciate what you're trying to do, Lazarus, but I really don't feel like talking about it anymore."

"Understood." Lazarus began banking the plane's nose downward. If his calculations were correct, they weren't far from the entrance to the interior world of Vorium.

"Look!" Samantha said, pointing at something in the snow and ice. Lazarus saw it, too -- a military-style truck, parked before a large glacier.

"I'd say that's a good sign that we're on the right track." Movement near the truck drew his attention and he continued to bring the plane in for a landing as he began to make out that the movement came from two men, dressed in parkas. One of them was hefting something up onto his shoulder and pointing it straight at the plane... "Oh, no," Lazarus whispered.

Samantha saw it but unlike her employer, she hadn't recognized what it was. "Lazarus...?"

The rocket-powered weapon looked similar to the ones used by military forces around the world, but it was seemingly made of slightly different metals and design. Nonetheless, it was unmistakably a bazooka -- a rocket-powered weapon capable of sending a shaped-charge warhead capable of blowing their aircraft to smithereens.

The bazooka flared to life and Lazarus saw its deadly payload streaking towards them. He tried to pull hard the plane hard to the left, hoping to avoid contact with the shell... but it was too little, too late.

The plane exploded in a deadly fireball, splitting in half. Shards of flaming metal -- along with the plane's human cargo -- flew towards an icy demise.

CHAPTER XII
TWO KINDS OF SUFFERING:
LIVING AND DYING

EUN JIWON OPENED his eyes, feeling like the inside of his skull was stuffed with cotton. His mouth was dry, and he ached in dozens of places... and it only took a few seconds for him to realize that he was in a hospital bed, an IV line attached to his arm.

Memories began to flood back into his mind's eye... of his trek to 666 Holder Way, of his encounter with Eidolon... and with the sharp pain of bullets piercing his flesh.

He turned his head slowly, fighting off a wave of nausea and recognized his surroundings. He was back at Robeson Avenue, in Dr. Hancock's medical bay. The fact that he was still alive at all was amazing, given that he knew he must have been shot multiple times at close range -- and Jakob was a good enough shot that all of those bullets would have gone exactly where he'd wanted them to.

After craning his neck as far as it would go, he noticed that he wasn't alone. His boyfriend Eddie was seated nearby, snoozing rather loudly. Eddie was a dock worker and had been Eun's lover and friend for several years now... he looked exhausted and his clothes were rumpled. Eun wondered how long Eddie had been waiting by his side and he felt a twinge of guilt for their recent fights.

"Eddie...?" he asked. It hurt to talk, and his voice sounded like dry sandpaper.

Eddie sat up with a start and his handsome face broke out into a grin as he moved to stand at Eun's side. Their hands immediately closed around one another's. "Eun! I've been scared to death!"

"How long...?"

"A couple of days. It was really touch and go for a while there. Hancock was worried you wouldn't survive the removal of the bullets. It's a miracle that you're still alive."

"Lazarus..."

"He and the others went after Murder Unlimited -- and now they're in France at Mer de Glace."

Eun blinked in confusion. Why the hell would everybody in France? He was familiar with Mer de Glace - it was a valley glacier located on the Northern slopes of Mont Blanc massif in the French Alps. He and Eddie had joked about taking a vacation to the Alps a few years before Hitler had turned all of Europe upside down and he remembered reading a vivid description of Mer de Glace: "I can no otherwise convey to you an image of this body of ice, broken into irregular ridges and deep chasms than by comparing it to waves instantaneously frozen in the midst of a violent storm[10]."

"I need to go help them," Eun muttered. He tried to rise but quickly lay back down.

"You're in no shape to do anything but rest," Eddie replied. "Now stay still while I go get the doctor. If you try to get out of this bed again, I'll pop you one. Understand?"

Sighing, Eun gave a nod. He waited a few seconds after Eddie was gone before he yanked the IV out of his arm and swung his legs over the edge of the bed. He felt dizzy and sick to his stomach, but he refused to be an invalid while his friends were off facing Murder Unlimited.

Moving as quickly as his aching body would allow, Eun shuffled over to a small closet. Cursing, he saw that none of his clothes were there -- he wondered if they'd been so blood-stained that someone had simply decided to throw him out. He hoped not - he'd been wearing his favorite pair of trousers when he'd gotten shot.

"What the hell do you think you're doing?"

Eun spun about and immediately regretted the sudden move. It had been Eddie that had asked him the question and his boyfriend's expression was one of incredulous fury. Dr. Hancock rushed towards Eun and he steered him back to the bed.

10   William Coxe, 1777

"Eddie's right, Eun, you can't be doing this. You're in no condition to walk and if you insist on trying, I'm going to sedate you!"

"You wouldn't," Eun replied in a croak.

"Try me."

Eun frowned but didn't resist as Hancock pulled the sheet over his body and reattached the IV drip. "I have to help Lazarus," he said petulantly.

Eddie wasn't having any of it. "You think you'd be helping him like this? You'd get yourself killed and slow everybody down even if you did make it to France. Speaking of which, how were you going to manage that? They took the plane."

"I would have figured something out."

"I bet you would have." Eddie placed a hand on Eun's leg. "I love you, Eun. Just for once, listen to me and the doctor, okay?"

Eun agreed, though Eddie could see how hard it was for him to do so.

Eddie gave his lover's leg a pat. "They're probably kicking ass right now. They'll be fine."

ABBY HEARD THE tearing of metal and the screaming of the wind past her ears… she wasn't sure if her friends were alive or dead but until she saw their corpses, she wasn't going to lose hope. As her body hurtled to the icy ground below, she twisted around until she was falling face-first. She then shoved her palms outward, generating enough magical energy to slow her descent. She ended up being able to swing her lower body so that she landed softly on her feet.

Her relief was short-lived, however. All around her fell pieces of the plane and some of them were large enough to have broken her body. She sprinted towards the mountain, putting her hands above her hand so she could produce a small force field, just large enough to protect her skull. It was a good thing she did, too, as she knew that shrapnel was bouncing off the field.

Throwing herself into a small grotto, she was pleased to see that someone else had found the same hiding place: Morgan was there, looking only slightly the worse for wear. His tie had been sheared in half and his jacket was torn in several places but otherwise he was unharmed.

Morgan grabbed her by the arms and shouted, "Look behind you!"

Abby turned and her mouth fell open. Thrúd was standing out there, stared straight up with her hammer raised high. She was shooting lightning from her father's weapon, the bolts striking the larger pieces of the plane and breaking them into smaller chunks that nonetheless shook the ground when they landed. At her feet, stirring but obviously barely conscious was Samantha.

Thrúd finally lowered her hammer and reached down with her free hand to easily lift up Samantha. She set the blonde up on her feet and helped steady her.

Abby and Morgan crawled from the grotto, staggering towards the daughter of Thor. Morgan looked around for the men that had fired the bazooka at them but there was no sight of them. While he was glancing about, he spotted Lazarus and Bob -- the two men were investigating the parked military truck and Morgan felt a little embarrassed that while he'd been hiding for safety, they'd had the presence of mind to continue the investigation.

"Is everyone alright?" Abby yelled.

"My head feels like an elephant has been tapdancing on it," Samantha muttered.

Abby stepped up to her and examined a bump that was forming on her friend's forehead. "Give me a few minutes and I'll have recovered enough to try and heal you."

"Save your energy," Samantha said, wincing as Abby's fingers touched her head. "I'll be fine - and we'll probably need you to have your magic ready for whatever comes next."

Morgan concurred, saying, "These guys fired a bazooka at us! Can't wait to see what they have waiting once we actually reach Vorium."

Abby said, "What worries me is those guys weren't wearing the Murder Unlimited jumpsuits we've seen before. I bet they're actually Vorium citizens - and that means we might be headed into a trap."

"So, it's another day at the office, right?" Samantha said wryly.

"I mean, every place we go has people wanting to kill us so why should this be any different."

Lazarus and The Black Terror joined their comrades and the team's leader said, "We're close - the entry to Vorium is not far from here."

"Find anything in the truck?" Morgan asked.

"Nothing," Lazarus replied.

Morgan caught a flicker of surprise on Bob's face and he immediately knew that Lazarus had just lied to him… they *had* found something interesting in the truck but for whatever reason, Lazarus didn't want to share the details. Bob hadn't known that Lazarus was going to keep it quiet and in that brief moment, he'd let it slip with his features.

Morgan glanced about, seeing that no one else had caught the moment the way he had. Rather than calling Lazarus out, he decided to go along with it. He trusted no one in the world more than Lazarus so if he had his reasons for lying, Morgan was sure they good ones.

Lazarus looked around the group and asked, "Is everyone up to this? If you're not, you can stay here with the truck."

Morgan shrugged. "My ankle hurts, and Samantha's got a grapefruit growing on her forehead, but I don't think you could keep either of us from coming with you."

With a pleased expression, Lazarus drew his .357 Smith & Wesson Magnum and turned to lead the way to Vorium. "Then let's do this, shall we?"

THE PASSAGEWAY WAS very dark, but Abby was able to lead the way with her hand held high, blue flame licking along her flesh. It felt like they were descending into the earth for miles, but Lazarus was confident that they'd traveled no more than one mile at the most when his keen ears caught the sound of movement up ahead. It sounded like sharp nails on stone, accompanied by heavy-breathing chuffs.

Lazarus reached out and touched Abby's shoulder, bringing her to a halt. Without a word, Lazarus gestured for The Black Terror and Thrúd to move to the front and they did so with obvious relish. Despite the fact that Bob often seemed quite taciturn, he was quite fond of fisticuffs and often seemed to be most happy in the midst of combat. Thrúd seemed to much the same as her full lips parted in a grin as she stepped into the gloom.

The sounds of sharp nails on the cave floor grew much closer and it was obvious that something was now running towards them. As it came into view, The Black Terror gasped in recognition: it was a dinosaur of some kind, about the size of a large turkey - it had a long tail that was being held straight out behind it and its forelimbs ended in three strongly curved claws.

"What is that?" Samantha asked with a nervous tone to her voice.

"Velociraptor mongoliensis," Lazarus said - a species first uncovered in 1923 and named in '24."

Thrúd shook her head, not understanding why her companions were taking the time to name the beast. It was a monster... and monsters deserved only one response. She swung her mighty hammer and caught the creature on the underside of its jaw. The blow was strong enough to part the raptor's skull from its neck. Blood erupted, soaking Thrúd from head to foot and the warrior woman laughed in response.

"That was over fast," Samantha said, relaxing a bit.

Her relief was short-lived as two more of the raptors came streaking towards them. The Black Terror drew back a fist and punched one of the raptors right in its face. Teeth shattered and the beast let out a howl of pain, shaking its head and backing away.

The other raptor launched itself at Thrúd and raked the woman with her claws, drawing blood across her chest and upper stomach. Then the creature sprang away from her snapping its razor-sharp teeth at Abby. She barely missed the brunette's left arm and the confusion was enough to cause the blue flame to flicker out, plunging the tunnel into a stygian blackness.

Pandemonium broke out as those with guns were too afraid to fire them in the dark, lest they accidentally shoot one another. Lazarus felt the creature rush past him, and he reached out to snag the raptor by the tail. He gave it a hearty yank and felt the creature twist around to bite at him. Releasing its tail, Lazarus wrapped both hands about the thing's neck and held on tight. "Bob! It's in my grip!"

The Black Terror whirled about and felt the disturbance in the air in front of him. Lazarus began whispering, spouting nonsense words so that Bob could gauge the distance between them. He clenched his hands into fists and timed it, hoping that he wouldn't make a mistake and accidentally clock his employer.

His aim was true. His fist slammed hard into the side of the raptor's head, rattling its brains. The creature slumped in Gray's grip, its body spasming as it entered its death throes.

Abby reignited the flame around her hand and the entire group stared down at the corpses of creatures that should have died out millions of years before.

"Impossible," Morgan murmured. "How the hell could things like this have survived down here?"

"Vorium lies just ahead," Lazarus pointed out. "If a race of humans could have survived beneath the earth, why not other creatures?"

"What are those things around the creatures' necks?" Thrúd asked.

Lazarus knelt and pushed one of raptors onto its back -- and he clearly saw a leather strap buckled about its neck, with a small silver charm attached to it. He was reading the German text inscribed on the charm when he said, "These creatures were pets... trained to attack upon command. Each of them has a collar with their name on it. The one that Thrúd killed was named Scheusal."

"Wonderful," Morgan said. "So, we have to worry about super-Nazis, Murder Unlimited *and* trained attack-dinos.'"

"We know it's not going to be easy," Abby said testily. "Whining about it won't do us any good. What I want to know is what we plan to do about Jakob... are we going to give him a chance to explain himself?"

"He nearly killed Eun," Morgan replied. "I know you're sweet on him, but we can't forget that... or forgive it."

"Lazarus thinks Jakob might have deliberately avoided killing him," Abby said.

Morgan shrugged. "So, he just wanted to put Eun in a coma instead of killing him quick? Well, now, that changes everything, doesn't it? Let's throw our arms around him and thank him for being so great about it all, right?"

"Don't patronize me."

"No, your original question was a good one -- what *is* the plan, Lazarus? We need to know... because if you leave it up to me, I'm going to give him just what he gave Eun: three bullets in the chest."

Abby waved her flaming hand near Morgan's face and he took a step back to avoid being singed. "Jakob always told me that we'd never really fit in with you -- you, Samantha and Eun are the original Three Musketeers, aren't you? Everybody's joined Assistance Unlimited since then is always a little bit of a second-rater as far as you're concerned."

Samantha stepped between Samantha and Abby holding up a hand in front of each. "Let's not say anything we're going to regret, guys."

"Samantha's right," Lazarus said. Though he spoke softly, his words seemed to carry enough weight that everyone fell silent and looked in his direction. "In some ways, we're going to let Jakob determine the route we're going to take. My hope is to give him the opportunity to tell us why he's with these people and what happened with Eun... if he's truly gone off the deep end, we'll lock him up in Tartarus. But we're not killers by nature and I don't want any one of us their emotions force them to do things that would haunt them later. Our primary focus is on stopping Nemesis not on taking revenge."

"You can't imagine how glad I am to hear you say that - if there's one thing I can't abide, it's a murderer."

Lazarus and his companions all whirled about to see a silhouetted figure standing behind them, blocking their back up the path. No one could make out their features until Abby took two steps closer to the figure and her blue flame illuminated the mysterious arrival.

Even the unflappable Lazarus Gray seemed somewhat taken aback by the identity of the man standing before them... but it was Morgan that put the group's overall response into one single word:

"Well, damn."

CHAPTER XIII
TO DROWN THE WORLD

THE GOLDEN AMAZON stood outside a massive temple, staring up with visible loathing at a fifteen-foot tall statue that depicted some sort of awful Elder God. The statue's face was vaguely octopoid in nature, with long tentacles trailing down from a ridged chin. The body was misshapen and smooth, with two large bat-like wings protruding from the back. Overall, it was a nasty image and one that cemented The Amazon's opinion of these people in Vorium: she didn't like them.

"We are patiently awaiting his return."

The Golden Amazon looked over her shoulder, seeing an attractive young man with close-cropped blond hair and stunning blue eyes. He was wearing an outfit that reminded her of a toga and it revealed one smooth, broad shoulder. He smiled warmly at her and approached with obvious deference. "You should be careful about sneaking up on me," she said, though her tone was not unfriendly. "I have a habit of striking first and asking questions later."

"Yes, you look quite strong." The way he said it, she knew he was complimenting her. "My name is Josef. I hope you don't consider it impertinent, but I saw you from afar and I knew I wouldn't be able to live with myself if I didn't at least approach you."

The Golden Amazon looked back at the statue. She was always the aggressor when it came to sex but for some reason this fair young man was making her blush like no one ever had before. It felt both thrilling and terrifying. Seeking to regain control of the conversation, she asked, "So who is this... deity of yours?"

"He has many names," Josef said, moving to stand so close

to her that she could smell his cologne and feel the heat of his body next to hers. "He is part of a powerful pantheon that includes The Mother of Pus[11]."

"I have heard of her. So, this is a chaos god of some kind?"

"Chaos is the natural state of the universe. It is only through the folly of man that we pretend to have control of our lives."

"Strange words coming from an Aryan. The Fuehrer loves his bureaucracy."

"Adolf Hitler is descended from the same stock as us, but he is not our leader. We have evolved past the 'red tape' that defines the Nazi regime. Please don't judge us by the Nazis - we are so much more. And you - you are like every painting of the perfect woman I've ever seen." Josef reached out and let his fingers intertwine with hers. She allowed him to do this, wondering why her heart rate was speeding up so. His scent filled her nostrils and she felt herself moving closer to him.

Josef was leaning in to kiss her when someone seized him by the back of the hair, yanking him away from The Golden Amazon. It was Bushido and the Japanese woman shoved the Aryan away from them both. The man stumbled, looking shocked -- and angry.

He cursed at her in an ancient German dialect, but one look Bushido convinced him to accept the insult and leave the scene.

The Golden Amazon was incensed at first, but her head seemed to clear as the young man walked away... and she realized with concern that her strange reaction to Josef might not have been entirely due to natural attraction.

"He was using some sort of pheromones to control your mind," Bushido muttered, looking at the statue and shaking her head. "These people are not our friends."

"They're certainly not yours, are they?" The Golden Amazon asked. "When I rule the world, I'll make any kind of racial discrimination illegal."

"How magnanimous," the Japanese warrior said. "I've questioned a few of the locals and apparently they're all waiting for this god of theirs to return - they need a body of some kind to house its spirit. Thankfully, we're a few years ahead of their schedule or else they'd probably assume that Nemesis would be

---

11 The Mother of Pus appeared in *Götterdämmerung*

perfect, given the fact that he's proven strong enough to hold Loki."

"Did you notice how Müller-Murnau's eyes lit up when Lex mentioned the technology that would allow them to flood the outside world? I think that Loki might be influencing him… causing mischief."

"I agree. He's not the same since he took that god into his soul." Bushido sighed and turned to look at the surrounding city. "You and I may be the only hope for us to get out of here in one piece. I don't trust Eidolon and Nemesis… I can't predict his actions any longer."

The Golden Amazon knew that Bushido was right. The two women had bonded that night in her room and since then circumstance had caused them to realize that they had far more in common than they did with their male teammates. "Where is Müller-Murnau now?" she asked.

"Still with Lex."

"And Jakob?"

"I don't know. I was following him for awhile, but he lost me."

"I vote that we locate him and then track down Nemesis. We tell him that we're ready to return to the United States -- with or without him. Are you brave enough to do that? You have seed planted in your womb… you don't need him any longer."

"I don't want to leave him here."

"Because, despite your protestations, you love him." The Golden Amazon sighed and shook her head. "Men are the cause of so much strife in this world but the one thing they get right is their ability to separate the physical act of lovemaking from their emotions. You can enjoy sex with a man, but you shouldn't allow that to make you his slave. In the end, your own well-being should take precedence. If Müller-Murnau refuses to take us home, we have to go without him. I have no desire to stay here any longer than I have to."

"Eidolon," Bushido whispered.

The Golden Amazon followed her companion's gaze and she saw the masked man walking towards them. He stepped up close and spoke in a low voice, as if afraid that someone might overhear him. "We have a problem."

"Tell us," The Golden Amazon prompted.

"I did some exploring and then went to find Nemesis. When I located him, he and one of Vorium's scientists were touring the machines that controlled the flood weapons. I was watching through a window when it happened."

"When what happened?" Bushido asked.

"Nemesis murdered him."

—— ❦ ——

NEMESIS STOOD OVER the man's corpse, noting the rather beautiful way that the pool of blood spread out from under the man's ruined skull - it bloomed like a rose. He wasn't entirely sure why he had done it. The notion of killing the man had come upon him suddenly and he'd embraced it, seizing the pistol he wore under his coat and shooting the scientist in the side of the head. The man had been dead before his body had hit the floor.

The scientist had just finished explaining in broad terms how the machines worked - they looked like giant radio towers located under a glass ceiling. A flip of a switch and powerful waves would be sent through the ether, connecting with the warming machines hidden under the arctic ice. Within a full day, the ice would melt in such amounts that the water would raise ocean levels to the extent that flooding would ensue.

Stepping over to the controls, Nemesis studied them, a smile spreading across his face. It would be so easy to do it, to end the lives of millions around the globe. Yes, some good Aryans would die but so would many people that would have eventually stood in the path of Reich. It was a risk worth taking, he thought... and, besides, it would be *fun*.

That thought gave him pause. He had never been a man that had made snap decisions on the basis of how much he'd enjoy doing it... and yet, here he was, having just killed a man and now contemplating flooding the world.

All for the *fun* of it.

There was no reason not to indulge, he mused. He had the power of a god, after all... why should he remain loyal to the Fuehrer. As great as Hitler was, he wasn't the one that had bested

Loki, after all.

With a feeling of supreme triumph, Nemesis reached out and twisted the knob that activated the doomsday devices. In a way, he knew that he was fulfilling Loki's desire to flood the world and usher in a new age... but this time, it would be Müller-Murnau controlling the future and not the God of Mischief.

———

PHILIPPE HUYBRECHTS WAS just shy of his thirtieth birthday and he'd spent more time on the sea than he had on land. The son of a sailor, he'd begun accompanying his father on his voyages when he'd turned six years of age and he'd come to view the open sea as his true home.

Currently he was serving on a tanker that was passing near Greenland, standing on the deck and smoking the last cigarette that he owned. They weren't due to return to land for another week and he knew that the next few days would be hell as he tried to bum a smoke off the other crew members. On long voyages, cigarettes were as highly prized as the Captain's collection of naturist magazines - and those were considered highly valuable, indeed.

A large iceberg floated past and Phillipe was startled when a chunk of its tip suddenly slid free and fell into the water. The resulting waves sent the vessel rocking to and fro, leading to the captain rushing up from below decks.

"What's happening, Mr. Huybrechets?" the captain bellowed. He was a heavyset man with thick eyebrows and a weather-beaten face. Before Phillippe had answered, the captain had already said, "It's too hot. Do you feel it?"

Phillippe looked around, noticing that other chunks of ice were beginning to break apart. Now that the captain mentioned it, it *was* too warm, especially for this time of year. "I don't understand," he said, and he didn't mind how unintelligent that response might make him seem.

"This could be an awful thing if it keeps up, lad." The captain gripped the railing with such force that his knuckles turned white. "If even a small amount of the ice caps were to melt, it could lead to flooding in low-lying coastal areas. We need to radio the mainland."

Phillippe started to turn and head to the control room, where the radio was kept... but something caused him to stay where he was for a moment more. In a tremulous voice, he asked, "Do you think it's just happening here?"

"I hope so, lad... because if it's happening in other places, too... then we might be looking at the apocalypse."

———— ∞ ————

SIMILAR SCENES WERE taking place around the globe, as the major sources of ice began to melt in the rapidly warming waters. While it would take nearly twenty-four hours for the full effects of the warming engines to be seen, it was already visibly noticeable that the ice was beginning to break apart and the waters were rising.

The source of all this was hidden from sight, buried deep beneath the ocean, but if anyone had dived down deep enough to find them, they would have found large devices that were nearly twenty feet in length and some eight feet high. Composed of a particularly high grade of steel and plastic, the machines drew in water, superheated it and released it back into the greater ocean... and the effects were seen within minutes as the warming waters began to melt the ice that floated above.

As word began to spread, the governments of the world were uncertain how to respond... was this some natural event? Was it an attack of some kind by the Axis Powers... or the Allies, as some in the Axis nations believed?

As heads of state convened their experts in the sciences, the warming of the seas continued... and the waters continued to rise.

———— ∞ ————

"WHAT HAVE YOU done?" Eidolon asked, one hand drifting down to the handle of his gun. He had brought The Golden Amazon and Bushido to this place in hopes of finding Nemesis and they had found him -- along with the dead scientist, lying in a large pool of blood.

Nemesis turned to face them, and they saw a peculiar look on his face... he was smiling, a sort of rictus grin that seemed unnatural. His eyes were aglow, filled with a blue-tinged fiery light. "I wouldn't advise you to speak to me with such a tone again," he warned. "I think you might have forgotten who's in charge."

Bushido strode forward quickly, her boots making squelching sounds as they passed through the blood. She studied the controls of the machine and said, "He activated them."

The Golden Amazon drew her sword and pointed its tip at Nemesis. "The world will eventually be mine... and you have no right to damage it without my permission."

Nemesis looked at each of them in turn, his smile never wavering. He rested his eyes on Bushido last and asked, "You're not turning against me, are you?"

"I think that Loki is interfering with your thoughts," she responded. "This isn't like you. It wasn't part of our plan."

"*My* plan," he corrected. "All of you are here to be my foot soldiers, in case you haven't realized it. Beyond that, you have no power in this relationship. I am in control. If you don't like that, you're free to leave... but I suggest that you stay with me because only those that prove their loyalty to me are going to survive what happens next."

"And what is that exactly?" Eidolon asked. "What are you planning to do now?"

Nemesis tapped the side of his head with one finger. "In here, I've got access to Loki's knowledge. He doesn't like giving it up for free, but he doesn't have a choice. The longer he's in there, the more he belongs to me. He knows spells, rituals... when the time is right, when enough people have died, I'll use one of those spells to help shape the next cycle of the world. I'll decide what goes where and in what amounts. And if the three of you want to have a role in that world, you'll bow down before me -- and I'll make sure that the Amazon gets a few continents to play with and that Eidolon gets to enforce justice throughout the earth."

"And me...?" Bushido asked.

"You'll keep making babies for me," he said, adding a wink that only seemed to make his words all the more sinister. "I'll live a long time with Loki's help but not forever... I'll want a dynasty waiting to succeed me."

The Golden Amazon let out a roar and swung her blade, aiming to decapitate Nemesis in one stroke... but the Nazi caught the blade with the palm of his hand. Blood oozed down the blade and dripped to the floor, but The Amazon found herself unable to push her attack forward. He was too strong.

"I'm going to forgive you for that, Violet - but try it again and I'll lock you up and turn you over to Durok as a trophy."

On cue, the Asgardian servant stepped into view. He eagerly let his eyes roam up and down The Golden Amazon and laughed as she yanked her sword free of his lord's grip. Nemesis held up his wounded hand and let them watch as the jagged rip in his flesh healed itself.

"I summoned him a little while ago - teleported him from across the globe. I'm getting more powerful by the minute." Nemesis tilted his head to the side, listening to something that none of the others could hear. "You're all angry that we haven't killed Assistance Unlimited, correct? Then you're going to get your chance... they're here."

Lex's voice could be heard from outside, shouting orders to various people. "The guards say they've slain the raptors! Prepare yourselves! These people are agents of the enemy!"

"Can I count on the three of you to help me win this battle?" Nemesis asked. "We can discuss things afterward but all of you have reasons to see Lazarus Gray dead, whether it be hatred or simply because he stands in your way. We have the means to destroy him once and for all, here and now." His smile seemed to widen even more, threatening to split his face in half. "So... Murder Unlimited? Together, for at least one more time?"

No one said anything but one by one they nodded. The first to agree was Eidolon and the former hero turned toward the door without waiting to see the others' reactions.

The last to do so was Bushido -- and her eyes spoke only of hurt and betrayal. She glanced at The Golden Amazon and saw the same thing reflected in Violet's eyes.

First, they had to deal with Assistance Unlimited... but after that, Nemesis would have to be killed. There would be no negotiating with him - her lover was gone, having been absorbed into this strange mixture of god and man. Even if they could somehow remove Loki from his mind, they would have to deal with the Asgardian... so it made sense to simply slay them both at once.

Bushido let one hand rest on her belly, and she felt their child shift under her touch. Even if Paul was dead, he would live on through their offspring... and she would make sure that their child remembered him as a hero, not a physical shell for a mad god.

CHAPTER XIV
SENTINEL OF LIBERTY

WHEN IT CAME to being a beloved hero of the American people, there was one man that stood head and shoulders above the rest. While men like Charles Lindbergh and Leonid Kaslov had taken their turns as the nation's darling, it seemed almost inevitable that something would eventually lower the public's appreciation for their heroes - in Lindbergh's case, it was the revelation of his fondness for certain aspects of fascism... and for Kaslov, it was the simple fact of his birth as a Russian citizen in a world where America was increasingly looking at not just Nazi Germany but also Communist Russia with suspicion.

The one figure that had remained above reproach was a costumed man that called himself The Fighting Yank. First appearing in the early part of 1936[12], The Fighting Yank had garnered popular acclaim by smashing gangsters and saboteurs - as well as making many public appearances in which he espoused the ideals that had made America great.

The man that stood before Assistance Unlimited was undoubtedly that noble figure. He was instantly recognizable in his garb, which consisted of a domino mask, a tri-cornered hat, square buckles, white shirt emblazoned with an image of the American flag, blue pants and black shoes. A green cape with red lining completed the ensemble and while the getup might have looked silly on some, The Fighting Yank somehow carried it off with aplomb.

Lazarus took one step towards the man and asked, "What are

---

12 Comic book aficionados might remember that the Fighting Yank didn't make his debut until *Startling Comics* # 10 (September 1941) but as with The Black Terror, he appeared earlier in this universe.

you doing here?"

"Same as you, I'd imagine. I've heard rumors of a secret society hidden around here... and after spending a lot of time looking into it, I found tales of a place called Vorium. My sources said it was a nest of super-advanced Nazi types -- and whether or not we're at war with them, those Nazis are enemies of America and all that's good and decent!"

"Are you familiar with us?" Lazarus prompted.

"How could I not be? The famous Lazarus Gray and the brave men and women of Assistance Unlimited? The honor, good sir, is mine." Thrusting out a hand, The Fighting Yank gave a hearty handshake before saying, "Your roster has changed some, I see. Some old faces are absent and there's at least one new one."

Lazarus quickly ran through the introductions and then said, "I see no reason not to take your identity at face value so if you would like to join us, I'm sure we could use your assistance. A group of our enemies known as Murder Unlimited has found Vorium and they're led by a man that calls himself Nemesis. He's as dangerous as they come."

"Then I'll gladly give you all the aid that I can," The Fighting Yank replied with a smile. He was handsome in an all-American sort of way and he made Lazarus think of Middle America and traditional family values.

"Lazarus, I have a concern." It was Abby that spoke up and when Lazarus looked at her, he saw that she was staring at something just above and to the left of The Fighting Yank's shoulder. "Our new friend hasn't mentioned that he's not alone."

Samantha blinked in confusion. "I... don't see anyone else." She looked at Morgan, who intimated that he, too, saw no one besides The Fighting Yank.

Abby pointed to an apparently blank area near the roof of the tunnel. "He's got a ghostly companion. Fellow's dressed like someone straight of the Revolutionary War - he was on the winning side, it looks like. He's dressed in the colony's uniform."

The Fighting Yank stared at her in open-mouthed surprise and then he removed his tri-cornered hat, holding it over his heart and saying, "Ma'am, I am sincerely impressed. No one else has ever seen my ancestor. My real name is Bruce Carter III and the spirit you've seen is my ancestor, Bruce Carter I. He was a soldier during the War for Independence and was given a secret mission by none other than George Washington himself... unfortunately he was captured by the British, who put him to death and stole the plans that he was carrying. So great was the guilt that he felt for his failure, his spirit became trapped on the mortal plane... and he wandered the earth as a ghost until he became aware of me and my uncanny resemblance to him. He decided that I could be the instrument to redeem his soul. He appeared to me and gave the location of this hat and the cloak that I now wear. They're magically powered and give me superhuman strength and durability whenever I wear them. Ever since then, I've dedicated my life to protecting America's freedoms. I'm proud to say that I've done more than my share to keep us safe from those that would tear down Lady Liberty and plunge us into the crippling despair of fascism."

Lazarus could sense that his friends had more questions but he knew that those raptors had belonged to someone... whether they patrolled this tunnel normally or had been unleashed specifically to try and stop their arrival, someone was going to eventually notice that the beasts failed to return. "I think we can trust the Yank," he said, and his declaration mollified any concerns that that the others had.

"I'm honored," The Fighting Yank replied. He put his hat back on and gestured for Lazarus to lead the way. "Given that I'm operating on my own here, I'll defer to your leadership, Mr. Gray."

The group resumed their trek into Vorium but had only gone a few steps when Thrúd suddenly emitted a high-pitched squeal. She staggered against the wall, her grip upon Mjolnir loosening so much that the hammer fell to the floor with a loud thud. Before everyone's eyes, the form of the thunder god's daughter seemed to shimmer and diminish until in the end she was once more Sally Weatherby, looking quite embarrassed and foolish to be garbed in the warrior woman's attire. The fur and leathers were too large for her and hung loosely on her slender frame.

"Oh my god," Sally whispered. "I'm freezing - and half-naked!"

Morgan quickly removed his coat and placed it around Sally's shoulders. It did more for her modesty than it did for her warmth, but she smiled gratefully and held onto the garment with fervor.

Abby and Lazarus stepped over to examine the young woman and Lazarus said, "Bob, will you and The Fighting Yank please guard the tunnel leading to Vorium? Make sure nothing else comes chasing after us."

The two costumed men did as ordered, standing side by side and staring into the gloom.

"What happened to me?" Sally asked.

Lazarus looked down at Mjolnir and then reached for it. Unlike every other time he'd tried to heft the weapon, this time he was able to lift it with only slight effort. "Mjolnir has lost its enchantment. Without it, you've reverted back to being normal Sally Weatherby." Holding the hammer out to Abby, he asked, "Any ideas?"

"It's got to be Loki - or Nemesis, if you prefer. He must have done something."

To virtually everyone's surprise, it was Morgan that made the deduction that seemed to make the most sense. It wasn't that he wasn't regarded as intelligent, it was simply that matters of the supernatural weren't his strong suit. "I bet it's related to the destruction of Asgard," he said. When Abby gestured for him to continue, he added, "When Lazarus went there, he said the place looked like it was falling apart... the myths say that Asgard is utterly destroyed... the hammer was forged of Asgardian metal and drew its power from that dimension. If Asgard has finally broken apart, I bet the enchantments on things created there will stop working. Good news? Most of the weapons that Nemesis has probably won't be effective anymore... Bad news? Sally is just Sally now."

"But... the hammer unlocked her true self, didn't it?" Samantha asked. "How can she be turned back into someone that isn't real?"

Sally looked indignant but it was Lazarus that answered for her. "Just as Loki is currently housed inside Nemesis, Thrúd shared Sally's body with her... she was a human baby that Thor placed his daughter's spirit into. They're two souls in one body -- Thrúd said that Sally was still inside her after she'd manifested and I'm certain that Thrúd is now back in the recesses of Sally's mind."

"Yes," Sally said with a nod. "I can feel her there. She's worried that without the hammer she'll never be able to come out again."

"There's movement up ahead," The Black Terror said. "We need to get a move on."

"I'm just going to get in the way," Sally said, looking up at Lazarus. "Should I hide here in the tunnel and wait for you to come back?"

Lazarus shook his head. "Morgan, please take Miss Weatherby back to the truck outside. I think that would be safer than remaining here in these tunnels."

Morgan looked disappointed to be sent away from the others, but he didn't argue - someone needed to protect Sally and he knew that Lazarus wouldn't have chosen him unless he thought Morgan was the best person for the job.

When they had gone, The Fighting Yank stepped aside to let Lazarus resume his position at the head of the party. "Fortune seems to have smiled upon," the patriotic hero said. "You lose two warriors but gain one with the strength of ten."

Lazarus looked grim when he replied, "No offense but I'm not sure that Thrúd wasn't stronger than that... still, I'm glad to have you with us."

The company proceeded until the pathway began to grow brighter and the temperature began to rise. Eventually, they stepped out into the same clearing that had greeted Murder Unlimited earlier... only this time, the reception was far different.

Lex stood there with a full battalion of soldiers behind him. They were all wearing blue jumpsuits with black trim and were bearing guns of a design that Lazarus had never seen before. Several men held onto leashes composed of thick chains - on the other end of the leashes were more of the raptors and the men were straining to prevent the beasts from bursting free to attack the heroes.

"Welcome to Vorium, outsiders," Lex said. "Now prepare to die."

CHAPTER XV
PANDEMONIUM

THE RESPONSE GIVEN by Assistance Unlimited was swift and decidedly non-verbal. Lazarus gave a hand signal to Abby and the team's witch raised both palms and whispered a pre-prepared spell. Immediately a faint blue glow encompassed the heroes, providing them with a one-way force field. It allowed them to fire or throw things through the field but repelled attacks by those with evil intent -- preventing them from entering or firing through the field.

Lazarus and Samantha both opened fire upon the Vorium soldiers, felling nearly a half dozen in rapid succession. The Aryan forces responded in kind, but their bullets bounced off the force field, ricocheting in such a fashion that even more of the number were felled before Lex yelled for them to cease fire.

The Black Terror seized hold of a sizable rock and hurled it with all his inhuman strength. it slammed into the skull of one of the raptors, sending the wounded animal thrashing to the ground. This caused an uproar as the other velociraptors suddenly flew upon the injured creature, ripping it to shreds and fighting over the scraps.

The Fighting Yank took a moment to consider his options - he knew that he could do what The Black Terror was doing and find objects to throw at their foes but there was a finite number of rocks and things so he lowered his shoulder and ran forward, piercing the blue barrier with ease. He slammed into Lex, knocking the man off his feet and causing him to slam into the gunmen standing behind him. The group toppled over, and the others suddenly turned their fury upon The Fighting Yank. Because he was right in their midst, no one opened fire upon him for fear of hitting their comrades - for a moment, though, the hero vanished under a tide of attackers as they overwhelmed him by sheer force of numbers.

This turn of events didn't last for long. Bodies began to fly through the air as The Fighting Yank fought his way free of his enemies. As he delivered punches and powerful elbows to the heads of his foes, The Fighting Yank smiled and even found the time to whistle a few bars of the national anthem.

Lazarus grunted as strange star-shaped edged weapon about the size of his fist grazed his hip, leaving a red line in its wake. He blinked in astonishment as more of the weapons came whizzing past his head and he saw that several men dressed in a different shade of blue were hurling the weapons, which passed through the barrier with no ill effect. "Abby?" he prompted.

"They're magic-based," she responded. "The force field is designed to repel mortal weapons only."

"Everyone! Push through the enemy and reconverge at the base of that building to our left - the one with the sign out front!" Lazarus ran through the force field, right into the Vorium soldiers, and he blew the head off the first that blocked his path. He didn't bother waiting to see if the others were following his orders - he felt confident that they would without hesitation.

A hand grabbed Lazarus by the ankle, threatening to pull him to the ground. He looked down to see one of the fallen soldiers holding on to him with both hands... and Lazarus knew that if he were brought down now, all would be lost. Pointing his gun at the man, he fired twice into the fellow's shoulder. The soldier screamed and released his grip, allowing Lazarus to resume his sprint.

Bursting free from the crowd, Lazarus ran towards the building that he'd spotted earlier. He could read the sign now and saw that it read Ministry of Science and Defense in an archaic version of German.

A rush of noise from behind him led to Lazarus looking over his shoulder. What he saw gave him an extra burst of energy. The raptors' handler had free three of them and the monsters were hot on his tail and gaining fast. He thought about firing at them but he knew that he was unlikely to do anything other than waste ammunition if he fired while on the move - and he certainly didn't want to stop running until he'd made to his goal and checked to see if the door might be unlocked.

One of the raptors suddenly burst into blue flames, its body starting to twist about madly. It fell, tripping up another of its mates, who promptly hit the ground as well.

As Lazarus reached the Ministry building, he spun about and saw that Abby was the source of the blue flame, just as he'd suspected. The raptor that had not fallen was right in front of Lazarus and it leapt at him, claws and teeth extended. Lazarus raised his pistol and emptied it into the monster's midsection, grunting at its twitching corpse slammed into him, driving him back against the door. It gave way behind him and he tumbled inside, landing hard. For a moment, his ears rang, and he saw stars.

When his vision cleared, he rolled to his side and groaned. Placing his hands on the floor, he raised himself to his knees… and looked up to see Murder Unlimited looking down at him.

Lazarus had only a second to assimilate this before The Golden Amazon slammed her fist down atop his head, sending him into unconsciousness.

<hr>

ABBY SWERVED TO avoid the two raptors on the ground. One of them was still rolling about, his skin blackening as the magical flame devoured his body, but the other was scrambling back to its feet and looking about with rising anger.

Gunfire, laser bursts and animalistic snarls rose through the air behind her and she saw Lazarus tumble through the door ahead of her, knocked backward by the impact from a raptor jumping at him. Multiple bursts of gunfire ripped through the raptor and Abby felt certain that Lazarus had killed it.

"Abby! Wait for me!"

Abby spun about, recognizing the sound of Samantha's voice. The harsh words that had been spoken in the tunnel were forgotten now and she caught her friend as Samantha stumbled into her arms. "Are you okay?"

"My ankle hurts like hell, but I'll be okay." Samantha looked back to see that the nearest raptor was snapping and biting at The Black Terror. Bob reached out and caught the beast by the neck and he snatched it up, whipping it around his head before launching it at the pursuing Voriums.

The military force was in shambles now, many of their number lying on the ground in bloodied piles. Assistance Unlimited, though vastly outnumbered, had put a major hurt on their enemies.

The Black Terror and The Fighting Yank joined the ladies outside the Ministry building, both men panting slightly. Their uniforms were torn in various places, but both looked unhurt, though Bob's hair was severely mussed.

"Where's Lazarus?" The Black Terror asked.

Abby threw a thumb in the direction of the open door. "He's already inside. Did you guys notice that no one is chasing us anymore?"

The Fighting Yank stared back at the Vorium forces. Those that could were slowly picking themselves up off the ground and reassembling but it was obvious that they were not eager to resume battle with Assistance Unlimited.

"Oh, no," Samantha whispered, drawing everyone's attention. She was facing the door to the ministry building and when her friends followed her gaze, they saw Nemesis standing there with an unconscious Lazarus Gray held by the hair in front of him. Visible behind Nemesis were the other members of Murder Unlimited: The Golden Amazon, Eidolon and Bushido.

Nemesis spoke in a triumphant tone. "It's over... at long last, I've won."

MORGAN SLAMMED THE door shut and settled in behind the wheel of the truck. The keys had been left in the ignition and it was tempted to start the engine and turn on the heat but he didn't want to run down the gas in case they needed to use the truck later on -- after all, there weren't a lot of stations where they could refuel around here.

Sally was shivering beside him, pulling his coat tighter around her. She looked forlorn and Morgan's heart went out to her -- he'd always been a sucker for pretty girls with tears in their eyes.

Reaching out, he put a hand atop one of hers and gave it a comforting pat. "We're going to be fine, Sally. In fact, we'll be back home before you know it. Lazarus never lets anybody down."

Sally looked at him and, in the gloom, she looked more haunted than he'd ever seen her before. "It's not that I'm afraid -- well, I am, but that's not what's bothering me." She lifted up the hammer and shook her head before dropping it heavily onto the dashboard. "I was special when I was Thor's daughter... but I saw how disappointed everyone was when I turned back into plain old Sally Weatherby. How am I supposed to go back to being a secretary after all this? I have a goddess inside me and it's like a prison for her! If anyone deserves to live, it's her... I'm the one that should be locked away. I'm nothing. Nobody!"

"Hey, that's not true! Just because you're a regular person doesn't mean you can't make a difference. Maybe you'll stop some kid from wandering out into the street and getting hit by a car. Maybe you'll get hitched and become a mom and help turn out great citizens for our country - we certainly need 'em. Maybe you'll just live out your life being a good person and never saving anybody's life, but you'll still contribute by paying your taxes, putting a smile on somebody's face from time to time and being a nice person. Smashing bad guy's head in with a hammer or shooting them in the chest isn't the only way you can make the world a better place. If everybody just acted like decent human beings, there wouldn't be a need for Assistance Unlimited."

Sally sniffled a bit and then nodded. "Thank you, Morgan."

"I meant every word of it."

A moment of silence fell between them and then Sally leaned over impulsively and kissed him on the cheek. "You're a good man."

"Nah. I'm just a guy that's seen both sides of the fence... and being on the right side is a hell of a lot better."

A pinging sound made Sally jump in alarm and she stared with wide eyes as Morgan began fishing around in one of his pants' pockets. His hand came back into view holding a small radio-like device.

"What is that?" she asked.

"Short-ranged communicator. Let's us all keep in touch during missions… see this little screen on the front? In cases where we can't send a verbal message, we can hit one of the number keys and transmit a numerical message. Lazarus has assigned different meanings to each number."

Sally peered at the small screen, squinting in the darkness. "So, what does 008 mean?"

Morgan frowned. "That's just it… it doesn't stand for anything. Not anymore. A couple of months ago, Lazarus changed the codes. We use four digits now. This… this would be from the previous list." Under his breath, he added, "We changed it after Eidolon quit the team."

Sally blinked in surprise as Morgan got back out of the truck. He looked at her for a moment, standing just outside the door. "Where are you going?"

"This code… it means that we're in a critical moment. Lazarus and the entire team are down for the count. They need immediate backup."

"It could be a trap!" she pointed out. "And anything that could take down The Fighting Yank or Abby… you won't stand a chance!"

Morgan grinned and in that moment he looked years younger… his rakish moustache and well-tailored appearance suddenly appeared less fatherly and more like a hero, straight out of a Hollywood film. For just a second, it crossed Sally's mind that she should have kissed this man on the lips and not just on the cheek. She bet he knew how to give a kiss. "Sally, please stay here. It's time for me to go and save the day. I'll be back with everybody else in tow."

"Please, wait--!" Sally said but it was too late. Morgan had slammed shut the door and turned away from her. She saw him drawing out his pistol and checking to make sure it held a full clip.

Feeling useless once more, Sally locked both doors and huddled up tight.

※※※

"**T**HE WORLD IS flooding even as we speak," Nemesis said, striding back and forth in front of a prison cell that held all the members of Assistance Unlimited - and their newfound friend, The Fighting Yank. The members of Murder Unlimited sat nearby, watching their leader bask in his moment of glory. He'd promised them that he'd kill Lazarus and the others in just a moment, that he only intended to rub this in their faces for the sake of all those that had tried and failed to accomplish this very thing. "So, you see, even if you managed to get out of that cell, it's too late. You've lost."

Lazarus stood facing his archfoe, watching the other man through the bars of the cell. The bars were forged out of some kind of metal alloy unknown to him - one that was too strong even for Bob or The Yank to damage. Because of their unique properties, not even Abby's magic could free them from their metal prison.

"Is that really how it is, Jakob?" Lazarus asked, turning away from Nemesis and addressing Eidolon. The German stiffened when his former friend mentioned him. "Have you really decided to work with people like this? And Violet? I'd have expected better from you, too."

The Golden Amazon stood up, her eyes narrowing. "I will be ruler of this world someday, Lazarus… both you and I know that you would stand in the way of that."

"And you felt so weak that you needed their help to defeat me? I'm flattered, I suppose." Ignoring the way The Golden Amazon bristled at the implied insult, Lazarus looked to Eidolon. "Cat got your tongue?"

Nemesis stepped between them, blocking their view of one another. "They're not important. This is between you and me."

"Did you hear that?" Lazarus asked. "You three aren't important."

"They know what I meant," Nemesis replied testily. "Stop trying to change the subject… I want to hear you admit that I beat you. I'm better than you. Say it."

"I'm not going to lie like that."

Nemesis stepped so close to the bars that his nose almost brushed against one of them. His demeanor, which had been almost giddy, was quickly turning dark. "Why can't you admit it?

You've lost! You're trapped like rats... and the whole world out there is sinking beneath the waves! Your wife, your son, they're going to die."

"And what about *our* child?" Samantha asked. She stepped up to stand beside Lazarus and her eyes were as cold as the glaciers that were melting even now.

Nemesis flinched as if struck. He took a step back and looked at Samantha with a sudden realization that he might have doomed his child to death.

"Oh, I see... you didn't even think about her, did you? All that talk you gave me about how important she was and how you wanted to help raise her... but in the end, you're going to flood Sovereign and leave her to drown."

"No," Nemesis said, shaking his head. "No... I'll go and get her. I can do that now. I have Loki's power and I'm growing stronger all the time." He smiled somewhat madly and laughed. "Besides, Bushido is pregnant with another child of mine. She's going to bear me many more. An entire army of Aryan wunderkinds! With a Nordic god's power within me, I'll even be able to remove any taint that might come from her own heritage. I'll purify them and leave them as true Aryans!"

An animalistic roar warned Nemesis, causing him to whirl about. Bushido was rushing towards him, swinging her **naginata** with deadly intent.

What happened next was all the proof that Lazarus needed that Nemesis was telling the truth about his growing power. The Nazi threw up both hands to defend himself and an explosion of energy shot forth from his hands. Lazarus was fairly certain that it was an instinctive move on the part of Nemesis and not intentional - regardless, the energy slammed into Bushido and tore the flesh right off her bones. By the time her momentum carried her to the feet of her unborn baby's father, she was little more than a skeleton covered by gristle and red meat. The child that she had carried within her was killed instantly.

As Bushido's corpse dropped to his feet, Nemesis let his mouth fall open and for a moment, just the tiniest of moments, he was himself again... the man that possessed a modicum of decency had returned and he looked horrified by the murder he had just committed.

Then the moment was gone, and the insane, power-mad Nemesis returned.

He whirled to face Lazarus, his entire body beginning to glow. "That was your fault…"

Abby whispered, "Lazarus, get close to me before he attacks you. I might can protect you…"

Lazarus ignored her and said, "I think that rules out her bearing you all those Aryan babies, doesn't it?"

"I'll just take Miss Grace as her replacement, then… or maybe I should just claim everything that was yours and make Kelly my breeding mare." A twitch in Lazarus' cheek was the only indication that he was angered by those words and it was only noticeable to those that knew him well. Nemesis saw it, however, and was pleased. He twisted the proverbial knife once more by saying, "I'll even take your son and raise him as my own… but he'll always be treated like a little mongrel. A toy for my own children to beat up on."

A loud explosion rocked the prison and sent dust falling from the low-hanging ceiling. Nemesis looked about in confusion. "What was that?" he asked.

The Golden Amazon was staring at the smoking body of her friend and said nothing. It was Eidolon that said, "Want me to go and check?"

Nemesis glanced down at Bushido's body and he shook his head. He looked like he'd been rattled and hadn't fully recovered yet. "No, I'll do it." Gesturing towards the cell, he added, "This is the opportunity you two have been waiting for: kill them all."

Eidolon drew his pistols. "I figured you'd want to be the one to take out Lazarus."

Without a look back, Nemesis strode to the door and flung it open. "I've already won." In the time it took the door to swing shut after Nemesis walked through it, everyone heard screaming -- and gunfire. Then the noises were muffled but those closest to the door also noted how unusually dim it looked outside.

Lazarus stared at Eidolon and asked, "Well?"

Eidolon pointed his gun into the cell and replied, "This is where it ends, Lazarus."

CHAPTER XVI
MORGAN WATTS: SLAYER OF MEN!

MORGAN WAS SKILLED in several things: fashion, the wooing of pretty girls, marksmanship and breaking things. It was that last talent that had allowed him to plunge Voirum into utter chaos.

After sneaking back into the subterranean city - which Morgan found was much easier when he was traveling alone instead of in a noisy group - he had crept over to a large pen that contained several large creatures that he was certain should have been extinct long ago. He was fairly certain they were called triceratops but studying dinos didn't fall into that list of things he was good at, so he wasn't confident about that being accurate.

Once the triceratops started roaming free, causing a number of minor disturbances, Morgan had entered a building marked Geothermal Studies. The place seemed to operate mostly on its own because he didn't see anyone working there - there were just lots of very complicated-looking machinery humming along. Once he began unplugging things and smashing others, a number of small fires had broken out and he'd moved on to other acts of sabotage.

He wasn't sure what was going on with Lazarus and the others - for all he knew, they were in immediate danger. Unfortunately, he was a lone man with limited ammunition, so he knew that he needed to cause as many problems as possible to spread out the Vorium resources.

This was accomplished to the nth degree when he came upon a peculiar device that looked something like a large cannon perched atop a hill. It was pointing directly at the huge artificial sun that hung in the sky and the air rippled in the front of the "cannon's" barrel, telling Morgan that it was transmitting some sort of invisible ray. Was it powering the sun? Did it somehow keep it in place, preventing it from wandering about? Morgan wasn't sure because electrical engineering and science in general didn't fit into his skill set... but he figured he'd find out once he started breaking the device.

Indeed, the answer came almost immediately. The sun suddenly started growing dark and, even more impressively, began to sink towards the ground... Men and women throughout the city took immediate notice, with many of them standing and screaming. Morgan was grinning when several people pointed in his direction and he knew that his secret campaign of destruction had been outed.

Drawing his gun, he began sprinting down the hill, dodging bullets as he went. One of the shots exploded on the ground right in front of him, missing him by a foot or two at most. He didn't return fire, knowing that he had to save his ammunition as much as possible.

A group of three jumpsuited people were waiting for him at the bottom - two men and one woman. The three of them were armed with some sort of nightstick or baton but Morgan saw that the sticks were crackling with electrical energy and he knew instinctively that he didn't want to let those things touch him.

Morgan raised his pistol and shot one of the men in the left eye. The guy was dead before he hit the ground. Ducking under a blow from the other guy's baton, Morgan slammed his gun into the man's chest and shot him right in the heart.

That left the girl and she proved to be the most dangerous. She drove her baton into Morgan's kidney and his body exploded with pain. He couldn't even scream - his body began convulsing and he nearly wet himself.

He fell to his knees and she raised her baton, obviously intending to batter him to death with it. Morgan was half out of his mind with pain, but his sense of self-preservation told him to hang on and not pass out. He raised his gun and fired blindly, squeezing off three rounds. Two of the shots went wild but the third hit home in the woman's throat. She staggered back and fell over, clutching her bleeding flesh with both hands.

Morgan struggled up and picked up the baton by its handle, figuring out how to activate it with a control switch.

More bullets flew and Morgan realized that others were catching up to him -- but the city was torn by multiple threats now. The triceratops were rampaging through the center of town now and the sun was continuing its slow plunge - resulting in the city now looking as gloomy as a Sovereign City alleyway. It was only going to get darker if no one managed to reactivate that weird cannon.

Suddenly a gigantic explosion rocked the entire city and Morgan lost his balance, toppling over to land atop the still shuddering woman. He pulled away from her with a start, disgusted by the feel of her against her and hating how warm her blood felt through his clothes.

He looked around and saw that the Geothermal Building had been the source of the explosion. Huge clouds of smoke were billowing up into the air and Morgan found himself laughing despite the dangerous situation that he was in. Lazarus and all their friends had gotten captured but Morgan, all by himself, had potentially brought down an ancient civilization.

Morgan looked around and figured that he was safe enough for the moment. Most people's attention had been turned towards the explosion. He fished out his communicator and started to activate it, but he hesitated -- should he try an audio call to Lazarus? Or should he stick to the numerical codes like the one he'd received? And what was the significance of the fact that the code he'd received was outdated?

He was in the midst of thinking this through when he heard a familiar voice ask, "Why am I not surprised that it's another member of Assistance Unlimited? I should have noticed that the geriatric wasn't among them."

Morgan turned to see Nemesis walking towards him, a strange glow surrounding his form. Bits of blood clung to the man's attire, as well, and Morgan hoped to heaven that he hadn't killed the others. Raising his gun, Morgan pulled the trigger... and heard the click that meant he'd spent the last of his ammunition.

He tossed aside the gun and brandished the baton, thumbing the button so that it buzzed to life. "Where's Lazarus?" he asked.

"By now? Dead. Shot and killed by Eidolon. Remember him?

This is where Assistance Unlimited dies."

"It might be where we *all* die," Morgan pointed out. He didn't want to believe that Nemesis might be telling him the truth - somehow, one way or another, Lazarus and the others had to be still alive.

They had to be.

Nemesis looked up at the falling son, just as Morgan had hoped. Morgan lunged forward, swinging his baton with all his might. Nemesis moved with the speed of a cobra, however, and caught the baton with his bare hand. Electricity sparked as voltage rushed into the villain's arm but aside from a gritting of the teeth, Nemesis showed no reaction. He began pushing back against Morgan's arm, shoving the baton dangerously close to Morgan's face.

"Really?" Nemesis hissed, his breath foul in Morgan's nostrils. "The last, great hope for the world is a failed gangster? Things must be dire, indeed, aren't they?"

Morgan gasped, feeling his strength about to give out. If he held firm, his arm was going to snap... but if he let go, that baton would slam right in the middle of his face. He was fairly sure that another blow from that thing would either knock him out or kill him.

Faced with the potential that he was about to lose, Morgan reacted with the bravery that had characterized his entire life. As a mafia confidence man, he'd done whatever it took to survive... and with Assistance Unlimited, he had repeatedly put his existence on the line against threats that were much greater than he.

He turned his shoulders slightly and then slammed his forehead against that of his enemy. The blow was enough to stun Nemesis and he released his grip on the baton, which allowed Morgan to yank it free.

Knowing that this might be his only chance for victory, Morgan slammed it again and again atop his enemy's skull. Nemesis fell to his knees, blood beginning to drip from his nose. Morgan kept going, raining one blow after another. His face was bathed in a fine spray and when he paused, gasping from exertion, he saw that Nemesis' face was an unrecognizable mess.

Leaning forward, Morgan listened for sign of life but there

was no exhaling of breath.

"I did it," he whispered. "I actually did it."

His sense of elation was short-lived - he felt a sharp, ringing blow to the back of his head and then he was falling forward onto Nemesis' corpse.

Durok stood there for a moment, looking at the two of them before shaking his head. "Damn you, Morgan Watts. Damn you to hell." Turning his attention towards Nemesis' remains, he asked, "You okay in there, boss?"

A sickening cracking sound came from the broken form as his head lifted off the ground and his body swayed unsteadily as it scrambled back to its feet. The voice that came forth sounded hoarse and phlegmy, as blood had filled the voice of its owner. "Do I look 'okay,' you misbegotten beast?"

"Should I go and find you a new body?"

"There's no time," Loki wheezed. "I'm dying, too."

"But..."

"Listen to me!" Loki pulled Durok close. "Don't let them stop the flooding. The world must end... and you will be the one to shape the new world. Now pay close attention as I tell you what to do..."

CHAPTER XVII
THE RISING TIDE

PHILIPPE HUYBRECHTS FELT a knot forming in his stomach. They had sent back words of warning but to no avail... what could anyone do with the knowledge that the ice was melting and a great flood was coming? Grab your loved ones and head for higher ground? What if the waters continued to warm and that higher ground was suddenly not tall enough...?

He reached in his trousers pocket and pulled out a wrinkled photograph. It was a picture of a girl named Megara, a Greek girl that he had met eight months ago. They had hit it off right away and by their third date, they'd ended up in bed. She'd said he was her first, but he didn't really believe that... nor did he care. She was amazing and he'd actually considered staying ashore when the captain had called the crew back together for their next sojourn. In the end, the call of the sea had proven too much but sometimes, in the dark of the night, he thought of her raven tresses, the softness of her skin and the way she'd giggle when he'd run his fingers across her ticklish spots.

Looking up at the sky, he wondered to himself if this was truly a message from God. Perhaps he'd grown tired of watching mankind squander all that he'd given them... and this was to be his judgment.

Give us another chance, he pleaded. *We're not all bad... I promise.*

EIDOLON'S BULLETS HAD struck a specific spot on the floor of the cell and the assembled heroes had heard a strange clicking sound in response... and then the bars of the cell began to shimmer and fade away. Within seconds, they were completely gone.

"What in Washington's name...?" The Fighting Yank asked.

In response, the vigilante holstered his weapon and said, "There's a failsafe in all these cells, just in case someone was to get locked in by accident. They keep it a secret, though - only the highest-ranking security officers know about it."

"And how did you know about it?" Abby asked, hope visible in her eyes. She was desperate for a sign that Jakob had truly betrayed them.

"I tortured a man and he told me," was the reply. Eidolon looked at Lazarus and said, "I've been working from the inside this whole time. I sent a message to Morgan, telling him you'd been captured. Hopefully all that chaos out there is related to him."

"He's very good at breaking things," Lazarus said. "And Eun...?"

"I couldn't risk Nemesis finding out that I'd let him live - I had to make it look good. That was the 'proof' to everyone that I was on their side." He held up a finger. "For the record, I'm not one of you anymore and I don't have to take any orders from you. We just ended up working against the same people."

Abby took several steps forward and rushed into his arms. She gave him a hearty hug and he returned the gesture after a moment. "You're such an ass," she whispered in his ear.

"I appreciate the touching nature of this scene," The Fighting Yank said, "but we have other concerns. Is the world really being flooded? Does your friend Morgan need our assistance? How do we escape from here? And... what about *her*?"

Lazarus looked at The Golden Amazon, who remained near the remains of Bushido. "She won't stop us," he said. "She needs a world to rule, remember? She needs us to help save it." Turning to the others, he said, "Black Terror, Fighting Yank - go and find Morgan. Samantha, come with me - I want to see if we can figure out how to shut down or reverse the flooding process."

"What about me?" Abby asked.

"You go with Eidolon and The Amazon... I want you to cause such a mess that these people will remember us for a long time to come. It could be as simple as keeping them too busy to stop the sun from falling."

"The sun... is falling?" The Golden Amazon asked. She moved to the door and flung it open, looking up at the sky. Confirming his words, she asked, "How did you know? There are no windows."

Lazarus shrugged. "When we first arrived, I theorized that the sun had to be artificial and would make an excellent means of bringing down this racist wonderland... given Morgan's talent for mayhem, it makes sense that he would have thought the same."

The Black Terror slammed a fist into his other palm. "We have our orders, then?"

"You do. Be safe," Lazarus said... and then the heroes of Assistance Unlimited sprang into action.

THE FIGHTING YANK ran alongside The Black Terror, impressed by the other man's speed and strength. "I think you and I have much in common, my friend," he said. The patriotic hero dodged in and out of a small crowd of locals that were watching the pandemonium, never slowing down.

"I'm not sure that we do," Bob answered. "Aside from a certain similarity in powerset, I mean. You really know nothing about me, Yank."

"Oh, I don't know about that. I have a way of seeing through a man's walls and I can say that I like the cut of your jib."

The Black Terror slowed, and The Fighting Yank did likewise. Bob had spotted something lying in the grass and he moved towards it, regaining speed as he recognized the prone form on the ground: it was Morgan.

Kneeling next to his teammate, Bob felt for a pulse and found that Morgan's heart was beating strong. He carefully lifted the older man's head and found a growing knot on the back of his head. "Concussion," Bob murmured. He knew why Lazarus had sent him after Morgan - his background as chemist made him the team's de facto medic in the field.

The Yank stood near Bob's shoulder and said, "Nemesis is dead."

The Black Terror's head snapped around. "What?"

"His face look like someone beat it in with a stick." The Fighting Yank gestured towards another body lying nearby. Bob moved over and examined it, confirming that the Yank was right: Nemesis was dead. Scanning the grass, he picked up the electric baton -- the battery charge on it had run out but he knew enough about electrical engineering to recognize how terrible the weapon could be. "Morgan killed him."

"Then who knocked Morgan out?" The Fighting Yank asked.

"That's a good question," Bob replied. He bent down and lifted Morgan up off the ground, cradling the man against his chest. "Let's get him someplace safe."

After looking up at the falling sun, The Yank replied, "I'm not sure any place in Vorium qualifies."

<hr />

THE GOLDEN AMAZON wielded her sword like a scythe cutting through wheat - only it was human beings that she was carving up. She roared like a lioness and warm, wet tears stung her eyes and ran down her cheeks. It was weakness to mourn the loss of Bushido and she was ashamed to admit that she felt despair that she had stood aside and allowed Nemesis to kill the mother of his unborn child. If she could have gone back in time, Violet swore that she would have brutally slain the villain when she'd first met him.

Even had Lazarus not asked her to help sow chaos, she would have found a way to do so -- killing her enemies was a soothing balm for the open wound that festered in her heart.

She walked through the streets of Vorium, stabbing and punching anything that blocked her path - when a pterodactyl swooped down near her, aiming to make off with a corpse lying in the street, The Golden Amazon leapt onto the beast's leathery back, stabbing it repeatedly -- the creature tried to take to the air but Violet grabbed hold of one of its wings and ripped the flesh, causing the living fossil to screech in pain. Even when the pterodactyl lay dying on the ground, The Golden Amazon kept hacking at it - in the red haze that was her vision, she thought it was Nemesis that she was killing.

Abby and Eidolon lost sight of The Golden Amazon, but they were far too busy to worry over their missing ally. The two former lovers ended up standing back to back outside a Vorium security facility. As soldiers arrived for reinforcements or as security agents left the building to go render aid where needed, the duo attacked them. Abby focused on unleashing magical flame, setting fire to vehicles and people alike. Eidolon was seemingly always reloading and emptying his pistols, his bullets finding bloody homes in the bodies of his enemies.

Over the cacophony of screams, gunfire and explosions, Abby yelled, "I missed you, Jakob!"

"Are we really going to do this now?" he asked.

"Considering we might both die, why not?"

Jakob ducked as a soldier stabbed a bayonet towards his head. He shoved the barrel of his gun up into the other man's ribs and fired. "I missed you, too! I thought you wouldn't want to talk to me anymore after I left the team."

"Oh, please," she muttered. "You were just afraid I'd point out what an absolute idiot you were to quit in the first place! You let your pride get out of control, that's all." Abby raised both hands and unleashed a wave of magical fire that engulfed two soldiers and their leashed raptors.

"I didn't quit because I was chafing under Lazarus' rule," Eidolon retorted. "It was a philosophical difference!"

"None of us agree all the time, Jakob… but we're stronger together than we are apart!"

Eidolon lowered his weapon, noticing that there was a pause in the battle. The sun, which had steadily dropped during the conflict, was now rising once more and its light seemed to be renewing. Someone, somewhere, had managed to stop the falling of the life-giving orb.

He turned to face Abby, reaching up to peel away the skull-like mask that he wore. She saw his handsome face and piercing blue eyes. His hair was slick with sweat and she had to resist the urge to reach out and run her hands through it, smoothing away the stray locks that were falling over his forehead.

"What…?" she asked, seeing the way his eyes were searching over her face. The clamor fell away around them and for a moment she was acutely aware of the pounding of her heart.

"I just wanted to say that I love you, Abigail. I knew it before I left the team... and the time away from you only made that all the more clear." He reached out and touched her face. "But I'm not going to stay in Sovereign. I'm clearing out after this. Will you please come with me?"

LAZARUS AND SAMANTHA found their way back to the ministry building but rather than bursting into the facility, Lazarus paused outside the door.

The expression on his face made Samantha ask, "What's wrong?"

"Look at these." He reached out and traced several strange designs that had been etched into the wood frame of the door. Samantha hadn't even noticed them at first but now she took stock of them.

"Looks like Norse runes," she said.

"That's what they are. Perhaps Nemesis came back here..."

"Can you read them?" Samantha asked. She pulled out her pistol and moved the safety off.

"Looks like they're part of some ritual or spell but I'm not the expert on them that Kelly is." He gave a shrug of his shoulders and said, "We're not going to gain anything by waiting out here - we might as well ask him what he's up to directly."

Pushing the door open, Lazarus led the way inside. He held his .357 Smith & Wesson Magnum, his finger resting lightly on the trigger. The entire team had taken a moment to track down their weapons before leaving the prison and he was glad they'd done so. Given the power of Loki that Nemesis now possessed, Lazarus wasn't certain that his bullets would be enough -- but he felt better for having the gun with him, nonetheless.

The interior of the building was filled with strange whirring mechanical devices but those did not catch the attention of the heroes -- both of them focused their entire focus on the sight of Durok. The servant of Loki was standing in front of the device that controlled the flooding machinery and he had stripped off his shirt, revealing a torso that was covered in runes similar to those around the door.

"Welcome, Lazarus," Durok said with a grin. "Somehow I knew that it would be you that came to stop me."

Lazarus raised his pistol and fired - the bullet whizzed through the air, on an arc that would have left it lodged directly in Durok's throat. It began to slow as it neared the figure, however, and gradually came to rest in the air about ten inches from its mark.

Durok extended a hand towards the bullet and flicked it aside. It landed with a clank against the concrete floor. "There's a field of energy around me, Lazarus... you can't harm me, and I don't plan to lower the protective wall until after I've finished the spell."

Under his breath, Lazarus said, "Samantha, sneak around behind him. Destroy that machine." As Samantha began to back away, Lazarus raised his voice and asked, "What spell is that, Durok? It can't be too important if Nemesis would reply on you to carry it out... I mean, where is your lord and master, anyway? Hightailing it out of here?"

Durok's face twitched and he replied in a dark tone. "Loki is dead, slain by one of your agents."

Lazarus managed to hide his surprise, but he felt a surge of pride at the villain's words. He wondered which of his people had managed to kill Nemesis... he didn't feel any regret that it hadn't been him to do the deed, though. The important thing was that evil was vanquished. the hand that performed the task was not as important as that overall fact.

"I hope he died painfully," Lazarus said, hoping to further unsettle the villain. It seemed to be working as Durok was seemingly unconcerned that Samantha had now crept behind some of the machinery and disappeared out of view.

"He did with all the bravery that befitted a God of Asgard. He would not have lost at all had it not been the influence of his human host." Durok held up both hands, palm upward. "The world will soon be washed away and the spell I have running will allow me to shape the next cycle... and I will do so, as my master commanded!"

Lazarus walked closer, stopping only when he felt a change in the air around him. It began to feel *thicker*, as if the air was composed of invisible molasses. What's more, any place that his body touched the outer perimeter of this barrier, his skin burned. "Still not your own man, are you? Even with Loki dead, you're still carrying out his orders? This is your opportunity to become the master of reality... and you're worried about a dead man's wishes?"

Durok sneered, "Save your insults, mortal. You can do nothing to stop me."

Lazarus took a deep breath and pushed his arm deeper into the field. It hurt like hell, but he refused to quit... and then he walked forward, ready to put his body at extreme risk to reach Durok.

Durok lowered his hands and his eyes grew wide. "You can't make it through..."

Lazarus gritted his teeth and pressed on. The air was getting harder to navigate and the pain was intensifying. It felt like his skin was being flayed but when he looked at his arm, it seemed fine... the pain, he believed, was all in his mind. That gave him the additional strength to keep going... that and the thought of his wife and son, both being put in harm's way. Sovereign was a port town, after all, and it would be one of the first cities to flood when the rising waters reached the eastern coast of the United States.

Step by ponderous step, Lazarus crept closer to his foe. His entire body was now shaking from the exertion and a lesser man would never have been able to accomplish this task. It took all of his considerable willpower not to surrender, not to fall to his knees and scream in agony... but this was Lazarus Gray, who had been born as Richard Winthrop and had survived the deaths of his parents, the evil clutches of The Illuminati, and then even Hell itself.

He would not be bested by the likes of Durok.

Lazarus stepped up in front of the villain, panting and with sweat pouring off his body. "Stop the ceremony," he warned.

Durok seemed frightened and his eyes were wide as saucers. He looked at Lazarus with obvious amazement. "Impossible... you're not human!"

Lazarus gripped Durok's throat and squeezed with all his might. "The way I understand it is Loki revives you every time you die, right? If he's not around anymore, does that mean you can die for good?"

The fear in Durok's eyes made it clear what the answer was. When Lazarus loosened his grip, Durok suddenly sucked in a lungful of air and hissed, "The ceremony can't be stopped... it's drawing energy from me and won't end until a certain number of humans have drowned. Their deaths will release energy that will be absorbed back into me and then I can shape it."

With a sigh of regret, Lazarus reapplied the pressure to the man's neck. "That's what I was afraid of. The only way to stop the spell is to stop you... permanently. I hate to take a life but sometimes it's necessary. I'm sorry."

Durok began struggling, punching at his attacker's midsection. He tried to writhe free, but Lazarus held firm, even as he felt his ribs beginning to bruise under the onslaught.

Energy swirled around them and Lazarus knew that this was coming from the deaths of innocents around the globe... it hadn't reached a critical mass just yet and neither of them would be able to manipulate reality but given enough time, that would occur.

It passed through his mind that if he held out long enough, he would be able to shape the world so that there would no hunger, no war... but also no free will. Those things were the unfortunate byproducts of allowing the human race to decide to themselves what their priorities would be. He might wish that they all shared his views but if he did that, he would be no better than The Golden Amazon - a would-be 'hero' that really was little different than those she fought against.

Knowing that there was only one way out of this mess, Lazarus drew Durok closer and, when the other man began to weaken, he used his grip to twist Durok's head to the side. It occurred with such ferocity that the snapping of the villain's neck sounded strangely loud, even amid the humming of machinery.

The invisible barrier - and the spell that was absorbing the death energy of those being flooded - faded with the spark of life that now ebbed within Durok.

Lazarus swayed and let Durok fall. All the strain of passing through the barrier now came rushing in all at once and Lazarus felt himself struggling to remain conscious.

Samantha's hands came around his midsection and he let

himself lean heavily against her. She grunted but held firm. "Lazarus, I busted up the machine. I hope that stops it."

"That's all we can do," he replied. "We have to help the others…"

"You need to sit down and rest," she said, and he didn't protest when she began helping him to the floor. He ended up sitting with his back against the flood machine, his feet mere inches from Durok's corpse.

"Someone killed Nemesis," he said. "I wonder who it was."

Samantha looked contemplative and then her pretty face split in a grin. "Are you kidding? It had to be Morgan. That guy can ruin anything - even the plans of somebody that's your twin."

One corner of Lazarus' mouth lifted. "Are you sure you're okay with that? Like it or not, he's Emily's father."

"He might have been her father, but he never would have been her daddy. You and I both know that. She's better off without ever knowing him."

CHAPTER XVIII
HOMECOMING

EXITING VORIUM WAS a surprisingly simple affair. Lex and his fellow leaders were all too eager to be rid of the outsiders - Lazarus was able to get their word that they would not launch any retaliatory strikes against the rest of the world in exchange for Lazarus not completely toppling their civilization and dragging them kicking and screaming into the "mongrelized" world that the Voriums had fled from.

Abby was able to use her magic to send word to Kelly that they needed assistance and it wasn't long before another plane arrived to pick them up and take them home.

Morgan woke up with a powerful headache but the praise he got from his teammates on the return flight brought such a grin that the muscles of his face began to ache. Sally Weatherby sat beside him the entire trip, her father's hammer wrapped in cloth sitting in her lap. She listened with rapt attention as Morgan told - and retold - the story of his battle with Nemesis.

The Golden Amazon and The Fighting Yank accepted invitations to fly back with them though their reactions were quite different. Violet remained silent on the trip, staring out the windows of the plane and absentmindedly drumming her fingers on the hilt of her sword. Bruce, on the other hand, was quite animated, striking up a long-running conversation with Bob and Samantha about the merits of working with a team. It was obvious to all that The Yank, who had always been a solo operative, had been mightily impressed with Assistance Unlimited's loyalty to one another.

The remains of Nemesis, Bushido and Durok lay in the rear of the plane. It wasn't out of respect for the dead that Lazarus had brought them along - he knew from past experience that powerful magic could be used to reanimated the deceased and he wanted to make sure that none of those three would ever be revived.

When they settled on the ground at Sovereign International Airport, Lazarus was the first to step off the plane and he was greeted at the terminal by his wife and son. After a series of embraces, Lazarus asked, "How is Eun?"

Kelly laughed and said, "Up and about - in fact, we practically had to tie him down to prevent him from rushing to try and help you. Eddie is back at headquarters watching over him."

"Good to hear." Lazarus turned to look at the others that were disembarking and he held up a hand, gesturing for them to gather around. "Mind giving us a minute, honey?" he asked, looking at Kelly. She nodded and took little Zeke by the hand, leading him away so that her husband could conduct his business.

There would time for everyone to file an official write-up later, something that would go into the team's archive... but it was obvious that Lazarus wanted to get something out of the way first. She had a hunch that it might involve Jakob, since his departure from the team had caused a lot of stress.

When the group had assembled, Lazarus took note of their various demeanors. Some of them, like Morgan, looked absolutely exhausted and in need of a nice, hot bath. Others, like The Golden Amazon, seemed to possess a nervous energy. They constantly shifted their weight from foot to foot and there was that familiar, slightly wild-eyed look to their expressions.

"I wanted to take a moment to tell each of you that I'm proud of you," Lazarus began. He let his gaze lock onto each of them as he spoke, letting his vision swing around until it rested at last on Eidolon. He looked away, unsure what kind of response he saw in Jakob's eyes. "We encountered almost overwhelming odds, but we triumphed - and we did because of our various skills and abilities. Alone, none of us would have had a chance of success. But, together, we saved the world."

The Fighting Yank nodded and said, "The strength of the American people has always been in their ability to overcome their differences and find common ground. That unity is what makes us great."

Morgan leaned towards Sally and whispered, "Boy, that fella

never quits, does he?"

Sally stifled a laugh, hiding her mouth behind her hand.

Lazarus caught the exchange but pressed on. "We all know that the situations in Europe and in the Pacific are getting more and more tense. No matter how much we might like to think the United States can stay out of it, I'm not so sure... I'm thinking that we might need to eventually expand Assistance Unlimited beyond Sovereign - perhaps even going international. It's already common for us to travel outside our borders but I'd like to have members that live around the globe and that we can call upon to investigate problems that may not require the rest of the team."

Violet snorted and everyone looked at her. "If this is your way of trying to entice me to have some sort of formal alliance with your group, you don't have to go such extravagant lengths." She glanced at Bob and quickly looked away. "Our ultimate goals are at odds, but I have learned from the past few days that a lonely quest may be a wonderful one... but it would still be lonely. There is merit to companionship." The Golden Amazon flexed her muscles and said, "I accept your offer. I will answer your call when it is given, and I expect the same to be true of you."

Several bemused looks were exchanged among the others, but all Lazarus said was, "Fair deal. If the occasion arises that we need your skillset, we'll put out the call -- and you'll have access to our equipment and headquarters whenever you need it." He reached out and put a hand on her shoulder. "It goes without saying that you won't conquer the world without speaking with us first, though?"

"Assuming it doesn't just fall into place on its own, yes."

"That's all we can ask." Lazarus turned his gaze upon The Fighting Yank and asked, "Bruce, can we expect the same of you? Will you be on call when we need someone out in the field?"

The Fighting Yank took off his hat and held it over his heart. "I would be honored. What's more, you might find me accepting your offer of hospitality quite often. The backroads of America are beautiful but a place to call home would be nice."

"In that case, I'll see to it that you get a room to call your own."

Eidolon spoke up, his demeanor suggesting that he was weary - and not just from the physical demands of recent days. "Before you get around to asking me to rejoin, I'm going to go ahead and say that I'm not staying in Sovereign... and I don't really plan to continue with any kind of official relationship with Assistance Unlimited. This alliance just happened by circumstance. Besides, I'd rather not be around when Eun decides to get back at me for shooting him."

Lazarus nodded. He noticed that Abby had moved away from Jakob during her former lover's spiel and he wondered what had transpired between them. He had noticed them talking privately on the flight back and it sounded at times quite emotional. "Very well," he said aloud. "Just know you'll always have a place with us if you change your mind."

Samantha stepped forward and asked for everyone's attention. She paused a moment before saying, "I just wanted to let you guys know... I've had good friends and I've had family... but Assistance Unlimited is more than that. All of you are the ones I rely upon, the ones that I trust and... I love you."

Morgan raised a fist and pumped it slowly in the air. "Hear, hear."

Sally took a step back and watched as the friends began talking once more, this time all at once. She was aware that Eidolon was moving away quickly, and she also noticed that the shapely brunette - Abby - was watching him go. These people lived such amazing lives and she was glad that, for just a little while, she'd gotten to interact with.

Still, she was very much looking forward to going home and seeing her cat... heading into work... and returning to normality. She knew she was stronger than before, with the spirit of a goddess within her, but she'd be just fine without any more Asgardian nonsense.

Within the cloth that she held tightly in her hands, Mjolnir pulsed softly.

THE END

MUSINGS FROM THE AUTHOR

Welcome back to Sovereign, my friends. When I wrote the very first Lazarus Gray story ("The Girl with the Phantom Eyes"), I wasn't certain how well the series would be received or how long it would run. Nine volumes in, I think it's safe to say that it's become my most successful work, with spinoffs, crossovers and more to supplement the main volumes.

With this book, I wanted to both close of some long-running plot threads and also expand our universe a bit. Eagle-eyed readers who have studied our timeline know that certain things will be taking place in the decades following the one Lazarus and his friends are in currently and it's always interesting to try and make all the pieces fit. Hope you've enjoyed the additions of The Golden Amazon and The Fighting Yank to our cast of characters. I really like both characters and felt that, with some tweaks, they could fit in quite well with our existing universe. Hope you agree.

Look for our heroes to return in THE ADVENTURES OF LAZARUS GRAY VOLUME TEN: LAZARUS AT WAR.

Barry Reese
May 23, 2018

THE REESE UNLIMITED TIMELINE

THE REESE UNLIMITED TIMELINE

Major Events specific to certain stories and novels are included in brackets. Some of this information contains SPOILERS for The Peregrine, Lazarus Gray, Gravedigger and other stories.

~ 800 Viking warrior Grimarr dies of disease but is resurrected as the Sword of Hel. He adventures for some time as Hel's agent on Earth. *["Dogs of War"* and *"In the Name of Hel," Tales of the Norse Gods]*.

1748 – Johann Adam Weishaupt is born.

1750 – Guan-Yin embarks on a quest to find her lost father, which takes her to Skull Island *[Guan-Yin and the Horrors of Skull Island]*.

1776 – Johann Adam Weishaupt forms The Illuminati. He adopts the guise of the original Lazarus Gray in group meetings, reflecting his "rebirth" and the "moral ambiguity" of the group. In Sovereign City, a Hessian soldier dies in battle, his spirit resurrected as a headless warrior.

1782 – The man that would eventually be known as Gideon Black was born. *[The Second Book of Babylon]*

1793 – Mortimer Quinn comes to Sovereign City, investigating the tales of a Headless Horseman *[Gravedigger Volume One]*

1802 – Gideon Black's son is born and the chain of events that leads to Gideon being bonded with a suit of armor forged in Hell begins. Gideon is transformed into Babylon, a force for cosmic retribution. *[The Second Book of Babylon]*

1835 – Lucy Hale goes to work at Mendicott Hall. She meets Byron Mendicott and Lilith. *[The Chronicles of Lilith]*

1865 – Eobard Grace returns home from his actions in the American Civil War. Takes possession of the Book of Shadows from his uncle Frederick. *["The World of Shadow," The Family Grace: An Extraordinary History]*

1877 – Eobard Grace is summoned to the World of Shadows, where he battles Uris-Kor and fathers a son, Korben. *["The World of Shadow," The Family Grace: An Extraordinary History]*

1885 – Along with his niece Miriam and her paramour Ian Sinclair, Eobard returns to the World of Shadows to halt the merging of that world with Earth. *["The Flesh Wheel," The Family Grace: An Extraordinary History]*

1890 – Eobard fathers a second son, Leopold.

1893 – Eobard Grace successfully steals the Thirty Pieces of Silver that was paid to Judas for his betrayal of Jesus from The Illuminati. He melts the coins down into mystically-empowered silver and helps a friend forge these into bullets. They remain hidden in Atlanta, Georgia until the Forties. *[The Adventures of Lazarus Gray Volume 11]*

1895 – Felix Cole (the Bookbinder) is born.

1900 – Max Davies is born to publisher Warren Davies and his wife, heiress Margaret Davies.

1901 – Leonid Kaslov is born.

1905 – Richard Winthrop is born in San Francisco.

1908 – Warren Davies is murdered by Ted Grossett, a killer nicknamed "Death's Head". *["Lucifer's Cage", the Peregrine Volume One, more details shown in "Origins," the Peregrine Volume One]* Hans Merkel kills his own father. *["Blitzkrieg," the Peregrine Volume One]*. Abigail Cross is born in Tennessee.

1910 – Evelyn Gould is born.

1912 – Byron Mendicott travels to France to kill Lucy Hale. *[The Chronicles of Lilith]*

1913 – Felix Cole meets the Cockroach Man and becomes part of The Great Work. *["The Great Work," The Family Grace: An Extraordinary History]*

1914 – Margaret Davies passes away in her sleep. Max is adopted by his uncle Reginald.

1915 – Felix Cole marries Charlotte Grace, Eobard Grace's cousin.

1916 – Leonid Kaslov's father Nikolai becomes involved in the plot to assassinate Rasputin.

1917 – Betsy Cole is born to Felix and Charlotte Grace Cole. Nikolai Kaslov is murdered.

1918 – Max Davies begins wandering the world. Richard Winthrop's parents die in an accident.

1922 – Warlike Manchu tutors Max Davies in Kyoto.

1925 – Max Davies becomes the Peregrine, operating throughout Europe.

1926 – Charlotte Grace dies. Richard Winthrop has a brief romance with exchange student Sarah Dumas.

1927 – Richard Winthrop graduates from Yale. On the night of his graduation, he is recruited into The Illuminati. Max and Leopold Grace battle the Red Lord in Paris. Richard Winthrop meets Miya Shimada in Japan, where he purchases The McGuinness Obelisk for The Illuminati.

1928 – The Peregrine returns to Boston. Dexter van Melkebeek (later to be known as The Darkling) receives his training in Tibet from Tenzin. Sheridan Masters loses his fiance Carmen in a terrible mystic storm in Egypt. He is trapped in Carcosa for several years.

1929 – Max Davies is one of the judges for the Miss Beantown contest *["The Miss Beantown Affair," The Peregrine Volume Three]*. Richard Winthrop destroys a coven of vampires in Mexico.

1930 – Richard Winthrop pursues The Devil's Heart in Peru *["Eidolon," Lazarus Gray Volume Three]*.

1932 – The Peregrine hunts down his father's killer *["Origins," the Peregrine Volume One]*. The Darkling returns to the United States.

1933 – Jacob Trench uncovers Lucifer's Cage. *["Lucifer's Cage", the Peregrine Volume One]* The Peregrine battles Doctor York *[All-Star Pulp Comics # 1]* After a failed attempt at betraying The Illuminati, Richard Winthrop wakes up on the shores of Sovereign City with no memory of his name or past. He has only one clue to his past in his possession: a small medallion adorned with the words Lazarus Gray and the image of a naked man with the head of a lion. *["The Girl With the Phantom Eyes," Lazarus Gray Volume One]*. The man who would eventually call himself Paul Alfred Müller-Murnau arrives in Sovereign on the same night as Lazarus Gray. *["Nemesis," Lazarus Gray Volume Six]*.

1934 – Now calling himself Lazarus Gray, Richard Winthrop forms Assistance Unlimited in Sovereign City. He recruits Samantha Grace, Morgan Watts and Eun Jiwon ["The Girl With the Phantom Eyes," Lazarus Gray Volume One] Walther Lunt aids German scientists in unleashing the power of Die Glocke, which in turn frees the demonic forces of Satan's Circus *["Die Glocke," Lazarus Gray Volume Two]*. The entity who will become known as The Black Terror is created *["The Making of a Hero," Lazarus Gray Volume Two]*.

1935 – Felix Cole and his daughter Betsy seek out the Book of Eibon. *["The Great Work," The Family Grace: An*

Extraordinary History] Assistance Unlimited undertakes a number of missions, defeating the likes of Walther Lunt, Doc Pemberley, Malcolm Goodwill & Black Heart, Princess Femi & The Undying, Mr. Skull, The Axeman and The Yellow Claw *["The Girl With the Phantom Eyes," "The Devil's Bible," "The Corpse Screams at Midnight," "The Burning Skull," "The Axeman of Sovereign City," and "The God of Hate," Lazarus Gray Volume One]* The Peregrine journeys to Sovereign City and teams up with Assistance Unlimited to battle Devil Face. They also encounter a new hero – The Dark Gentleman. *["Darkness, Spreading Its Wings of Black," The Peregrine Volume Two and Lazarus Gray Volume One)]*. Lazarus Gray and Assistance Unlimited become embroiled in the search for Die Glocke *["Die Glocke," Lazarus Gray Volume Two]*

1936 – Assistance Unlimited completes their hunt for Die Glocke and confronts the threat of Jack-In-Irons. Abigail Cross and Jakob Sporrenberg join Assistance Unlimited *["Die Glocke," Lazarus Gray Volume Two]*. The Peregrine moves to Atlanta and recovers the Dagger of Elohim from Felix Darkholme. The Peregrine meets Evelyn Gould. The Peregrine battles Jacob Trench. *["Lucifer's Cage", the Peregrine Volume One]*. Reed Barrows revives Camilla. *["Kingdom of Blood," The Peregrine Volume One]*. Kevin Atwill is abandoned in the Amazonian jungle by his friends, a victim of the Gorgon legacy. *["The Gorgon Conspiracy," The Peregrine Volume One]*. Nathaniel Caine's lover is killed by Tweedledum while Dan Daring looks on *["Catalyst," The Peregrine Volume One]*, Assistance Unlimited teams up with The Black Terror to battle Promethus and The Titan in South America *["The Making of a Hero," Lazarus Gray Volume Two]*. Doc Pemberley allies himself with Abraham Klee, Stanley Davis and Constance Majestros to form Murder Unlimited. Lazarus Gray is able to defeat this confederation of evil and Pemberley finds himself the victim of Doctor Satan's machinations *["Murder Unlimited," Lazarus Gray Volume Three]*. Lazarus Gray is forced to compete with The Darkling for possession of a set of demonic bones. During the course of this, a member of Assistance Unlimited becomes Eidolon. *["Eidolon," Lazarus Gray Volume Three]*. Charity Grace dies and is reborn

THE REESE UNLIMITED TIMELINE

as the first female Gravedigger. [Gravedigger Volume One]. Dr. York attempts to revive Princess Femi so that she can aid him in battling The Peregrine *["The Peregrine Animated Script," The Peregrine Volume Three]*. The Dark Gentleman confronts The Shadow Court and brings them to justice. *["The Judgment of the Shadow Court," The Adventures of The Dark Gentleman Book One]*. A few weeks later, The Dark Gentleman learns the truth about Amadeus Crouch *["The Silver Room," The Adventures of The Dark Gentleman Book Two]*.

1937 – Max and Evelyn marry. Camilla attempts to create Kingdom of Blood. World's ancient vampires awaken and the Peregrine is 'marked' by Nyarlathotep. Gerhard Klempt's experiments are halted. William McKenzie becomes Chief of Police in Atlanta. The Peregrine meets Benson, who clears his record with the police. *["Kingdom of Blood," the Peregrine Volume One]*. Lazarus Gray and Assistance Unlimited teams up with Thunder Jim Wade to confront the deadly threat of Leviathan *["Leviathan Rising", Lazarus Gray Volume Four]*. Hank Wilbon is murdered, leading to his eventual resurrection as the Reaper. *["Kaslov's Fire," The Peregrine Volume One]*. The Peregrine and Evelyn become unwelcome guests of Baron Werner Prescott, eventually foiling his attempts to create an artificial island and a weather-controlling weapon for the Nazis *["The Killing Games," The Peregrine Volume Three]* Gravedigger confronts a series of terrible threats in Sovereign City, including Thanatos, a gender-swapping satanic cult and The Headless Horseman. Charity and Samantha Grace make peace about their status as half-sisters. *[Gravedigger Volume One]* Lazarus Gray teams with Eidolon and The Darkling to combat Doctor Satan *["Satan's Circus," Lazarus Gray Volume Four]*. Lazarus Gray battles the forces of Wilson Brisk and Skyrider. The Three Sisters are unleashed upon Sovereign City *["The Felonious Financier," Lazarus Gray Volume Five]*. Gravedigger confronts the twin threats of Hiroshi Tamaki and the immortal known as Pandora *[Gravedigger Volume Two]*. Lazarus Gray travels to Cape Noire to investigate the mysterious vigilante known as Brother Bones *["Shadows and Phantoms," Lazarus Gray Volume Five]*. The villain known as The Basilisk attempts to seize control of

Sovereign City's underworld *["Stare of The Basilisk," Lazarus Gray Volume Five]*. The Three Sisters unite with Princess Femi to combat Assistance Unlimited. Sobek's attempt to destroy Femi helps lead young Madison Montgomery into a role as Femi's handmaiden. Lazarus gets engaged to Kelly Emerson *["Immortals," Lazarus Gray Volume Five]*. Lazarus and Kelly are married. *["Wedding Bells," Lazarus Gray Volume Five]*.

1938 – The Peregrine travels to Great City to aid the Moon Man in battling Lycos and his Gasping Death. The Peregrine destroys the physical shell of Nyarlathotep and gains his trademark signet ring. *["The Gasping Death," The Peregrine Volume One]*. The jungle hero known as the Revenant is killed *["Death from the Jungle," The Peregrine Volume Two]*. Gravedigger, Lazarus Gray and The Peregrine come together to confront the terrible events known as Götterdämmerung. Many other heroes – including The Black Bat, The Black Terror, The Darkling and Leonid Kaslov are caught up in the events, as well. The insane villain Mr. Death is created. *[Götterdämmerung]*. Three months after Götterdämmerung, Assistance Unlimited battles The Librarian and adds The Black Terror to the team. *["The Affair of the Familiar Corpse," Lazarus Gray Volume Six]*. Assistance Unlimited journeys to Europe where they reunite with Eidolon and Abby. The group then teams up with a Berlin-based hero known as Nakam to battle Mr. Death and The Torch. Lazarus Gray confronts the spirit of Walther Lunt and Baba Yaga. *["The Strands of Fate," Lazarus Gray Volume Six]*. Mortimer Quinn is elected mayor of Sovereign City. Paul Alfred Müller-Murnau learns of his role as Nemesis and becomes an ally of Princess Femi and Madison Montgomery. Femi gains possession of the fabled Emerald Tablet. Abby becomes warden of Tartarus. *["Nemesis," Lazarus Gray Volume Six]*. Assistance Unlimited battles an out-of-control Golem and an agent of the OFP codenamed Heidi Von Sinn. Kelly's pregnancy takes an odd turn after exposure to an Aryan idol. *["Tapestry," Lazarus Gray Volume Six]*. Daniel Higgins bonds with the Hell-forged armor and becomes Babylon. His sister Stella is killed. *[The Second Book of Babylon]*

1939 – Ibis and the Warlike Manchu revive the Abomination. Evelyn becomes pregnant and gives birth to their first child, a boy named William. *["Abominations," The Peregrine Volume One]*. The Peregrine allies himself with Leonid Kaslov to stop the Reaper's attacks and to foil the plans of Rasputin. *["Kaslov's Fire," the Peregrine Volume One]* Violet Cambridge and Will McKenzie become embroiled in the hunt for a mystical item known as The Damned Thing *[The Damned Thing]* Assistance Unlimited teams up with Sheridan Masters to investigate a deadly alliance between Femi and a masked villain called El Demonio. The evils summon Hastur, the King In Yellow, and Lazarus is forced to travel to Carcosa. Kelly learns that their unborn child is infused with Vril energy. Femi and Madison Montgomery are both apparently destroyed. *[Lazarus Gray Volume Seven]*. Gravedigger engages in a war of wits with The King, a battle that leaves The Dark Gentleman dead and her forces in disarray. She uncovers the connection between The Voice and Nestorius – then stands for judgment before Anubis. *[Gravedigger Volume Three]*. Lazarus and Kelly Gray become the parents of Ezekiel Gray, Samantha Grace learns she's pregnant *["The Santa Slaying", Lazarus Gray Volume Eight]*.

1940 – Samantha discovers that Paul Alfred Müller-Murnau is responsible for her mystic pregnancy. Müller-Murnau forms a new version of Murder Unlimited alongside Bushido, Brick, Vixen and Alloy. *["As Above, So Below," Lazarus Gray Volume Eight]*. The Warlike Manchu returns with a new pupil — Hans Merkel, aka Shinigami. The Warlike Manchu kidnaps William Davies but the Peregrine and Leonid Kaslov manage to rescue the boy. *["Blitzkrieg," the Peregrine Volume One]* The Peregrine journeys to Germany alongside the Domino Lady and Will McKenzie to combat the demonic organization known as Bloodwerks. *["Bloodwerks," the Peregrine Volume One]* Lazarus Gray encounters Gravedigger and a heroine from another universe while in Istanbul. The trio end up battling an alliance between Princess Femi and a villain from another world. A loosely-affiliated grouping of female heroes consisting of Lady Peregrine (Evelyn Davies), Jet Girl, Fantomah and Kitten is formed. *[Worlds Apart]*. Samantha Grace gives birth to her daughter Emily. Assistance Unlimited battle a werewolf and free a young woman whose dreams are incredibly powerful *["The Girl That Dreamed," Lazarus Gray Volume Eight]*. Kevin Atwill seeks revenge against his former friends, bringing him into conflict with the Peregrine *["The Gorgon Conspiracy," The Peregrine Volume One]*. The Peregrine takes a young vampire under his care, protecting him from a cult that worships a race of beings known as The Shambling Ones. With the aid of Leonid Kazlov, the cult is destroyed *["The Shambling Ones," The Peregrine Volume One]*. Daniel Higgins and his sister Stella stumble onto a mob killing and Stella is badly injured. Daniel finds a strange suit of armor and bonds with it, becoming transformed into Babylon *[The Second Book of Babylon]*. Lazarus Gray and Assistance Unlimited travel to Kentucky to investigate the disappearance of a young girl. Eidolon quits the team after a debate about how to resolve the crisis *["It Wants To Kill You," Lazarus Gray Volume Eight]*. Nemesis and Bushido join up with the Occult Forces Project to resurrect The Speaker from the Stars. They are opposed and ultimately foiled by Assistance Unlimited and The Golden Amazon ["The Speaker from the Stars," Lazarus Gray Volume Eight].

1941 – Philip Gallagher, a journalist, uncovers the Peregrine's secret identity but chooses to become an ally of the vigilante rather than reveal it to the world *["Origins," the Peregrine Volume One]*. The Peregrine teams with the Black Bat and Ascott Keane, as well as a reluctant Doctor Satan, in defeating the plans of the sorcerer Arias *["The Bleeding Hells", The Peregrine Volume One]*. The Peregrine rescues McKenzie from the Iron Maiden *["The Iron Maiden," The Peregrine Volume One]*. Asgard falls and Thor's hammer ends up in the hands of his daughter, whose spirit is hidden away in the body of a young woman on Earth. Loki and his assistant Durok end up working alongside Murder Unlimited (Nemesis, Bushido, The Golden Amazon and Eidolon) to try and flood the world so that it can remade along Loki's wishes. In the hidden world of Vorium, Assistance Unlimited teams with The Fighting Yank to foil their plans. The Golden Amazon and The Fighting Yank both become occasional members of Assistance Unlimited. Nemesis and Bushido are both killed. *["The Sinking World," Lazarus Gray Volume Nine]*. In November, The Golden Amazon, The Fighting Yank and The Black Terror journey to Manhattan to team with Olga Mesmer to stop a plot by Doctor Satan and his consort (Lady Satan). The foursome remain together as The Heroes, an offshoot organization of Assistance Unlimited. The Black Terror agrees to serve as a liaison between the teams. *["Satan's Lair"]*. Tommy McDuff is injured during the attack on Pearl Harbor – he is taken from the military hospital by Eris, the Goddess of Discord. She gave him great power but at the cost of his sanity – as Phasma, he embarked on a scheme to use The Torch of C'thalpa to tear down many of the institutions of power. He worked with Rosemary Lunt (the daughter of Walther Lunt) and was opposed by Assistance Unlimited and Babylon. The villainous Billhook releases damaging information about Assistance Unlimited to the press. Lazarus Gray agrees to work with Major Caruso and Project: Cicada. *[Lazarus Gray Volume Ten]*.

1942 – The Peregrine battles a Nazi super agent known as the Grim Reaper, who is attempting to gather the Crystal Skulls *["The Three Skulls," The Peregrine Volume One]*. The Peregrine becomes embroiled in a plot by Sun Koh and a group of Axis killers known as The Furies. The Peregrine and Sun Koh end up in deadly battle on the banks of the Potomac River. *["The Scorched God," The Peregrine Volume Two]*. In London, the Peregrine and Evelyn meet Nathaniel Caine (aka the Catalyst) and Rachel Winters, who are involved in stopping the Nazis from creating the Un-Earth. They battle Doctor Satan and the Black Zeppelin *["Catalyst," The Peregrine Volume One]*. Evelyn learns she's pregnant with a second child. The Peregrine solves the mystery of the Roanoke Colony *["The Lost Colony," The Peregrine Volume One]*. The Peregrine battles against an arsonist in the employ of Bennecio Tommasso *["Where There's Smoke", The Peregrine Volume Three]*. The Warlike Manchu is revived and embarks upon a search for the Philosopher's Stone *["The Resurrection Gambit," The Peregrine Volume One]*. Joseph Williams is born (son of Mitchell and Charity). Assistance Unlimited is forced to work with Nakam and Lilith (leader of the

Crimson Ladies) to stop a plot formulated by a mystic named Woland and The Black Terror's archenemy, The Puzzler. The dead are raised in Sovereign City but Lazarus and his allies are able to eventually turn the tide with an assist from The Revenant and Baba Yaga. In the end, a shocking revelation is made that alters Morgan Watts' life forever. *[The Adventures of Lazarus Gray Volume Eleven]*.

1943 – The Peregrine teams with Xander to deal with the Onyx Raven *["The Onyx Raven", The Peregrine Volume Three]*. The Peregrine is confronted by the twin threats of Fernando Pasarin and the undead pirate Hendrik van der Decken *["The Phantom Vessel," The Peregrine Volume Two]*. Evelyn and Max become the parents of a second child, Emma Davies. The Peregrine teams with the daughter of the Revenant to battle Hermann Krupp and the Golden Goblin *["Death from the Jungle," The Peregrine Volume Two]* The Peregrine battles Doctor Satan over possession of an ancient Mayan tablet *["The Four Peregrines," The Peregrine Volume Two]*. The Peregrine travels to Peru to battle an undead magician called The Spook *["Spook," The Peregrine Volume Two]*. The Peregrine clashes with Doctor Death, who briefly takes possession of Will McKenzie *["The Peregrine Nevermore," The Peregrine Volume Three]*. Baron Rudolph Gustav gains possession of the Rod of Aaron and kidnaps Evelyn, forcing the Peregrine into an uneasy alliance with the Warlike Manchu *["Dead of Night," The Peregrine Volume Two]*. Doctor Satan flees to the hidden land of Vorium, where the Peregrine allies with Frankenstein's Monster to bring him to justice *["Satan's Trial," The Peregrine Volume Two]*. Tim Roland is recruited by The Flame and Miss Masque *["The Ivory Machine," The Peregrine Volume Two]*. The Black Terror investigates a German attempt to replicate his powers and becomes friends with a scientist named Clarke *["Terrors", The Peregrine Volume Two]*. Assistance Unlimited and The Heroes come together to work with L'Homme Fantastique in returning Lazarus Gray to normalcy. El Demonio and a return visit to Carcosa are involved *[Lazarus Gray Volume 12]*. Rama-Memnon, Teddy Pumpkins, and Rose Dorcas lay waste to Sovereign City but are defeated by the combined forces of

Assistance Unlimited, Nature Boy, Eidolon and Wynona Jones. *[Lazarus Gray Volume 13]*.

1944 – The Peregrine organizes a strike force composed of Revenant, Frankenstein's Monster, Catalyst and Esper. The group is known as The Claws of the Peregrine and they take part in two notable adventures in this year: against the diabolical Mr. Dee and then later against an alliance between Doctor Satan and the Warlike Manchu *["The Diabolical Mr. Dee" and "A Plague of Wicked Men", The Peregrine Volume Two]*.

1946 – The Peregrine discovers that Adolph Hitler is still alive and has become a vampire in service to Dracula. In an attempt to stop the villains from using the Holy Lance to take over the world, the Peregrine allies with the Claws of the Peregrine, a time traveler named Jenny Everywhere, a thief called Belladonna and Leonid Kaslov. The villains are defeated and Max's future is revealed to still be in doubt. Events shown from 2006 on are just a possible future. The Peregrine also has several encounters with a demonically powered killer known as Stickman. *["The Devil's Spear," The Peregrine Volume Two]*. The Peregrine encounters a madman named Samuel Garibaldi (aka Rainman) and his ally, Dr. Gottlieb Hochmuller. The Peregrine and his Claws team defeat the villainous duo and several new heroes join the ranks of the Claws team — Miss Masque, Black Terror & Tim and The Flame. *["The Ivory Machine," The Peregrine Volume Two]*

1948 — SIGIL (Supreme International Group for Illegal Liaisons) is formed out of the remnants of the Nazis and The Illuminati. *[Assistance Unlimited: The Silver Age – Broken Empire]*

1953 – The Peregrine acquires the Looking Glass from Lu Chang. *["Black Mass," The Peregrine Volume One]*

1961 – Max's son William becomes the second Peregrine. *["The Four Peregrines," The Peregrine Volume Two]*

1964 – Mitchell Williams passes away from cancer. Charity

Grace is invited to join Assistance Unlimited by her niece, Emily. *[Gravedigger Volume Three]*. Benjamin Falk, a former Secret Service Agent, is recruited into Assistance Unlimited. Alongside Emily Grace, Sato Shinji, Ezekiel Gray and Bart Hill, he assists in defeating an attempted Fourth Reich led by Marvin Levin and his clone army. Emily and Ezekiel then lead a battle with the forces of SIGIL (Supreme International Group for Illegal Liaisons) and a would-be god named Helios. *[Assistance Unlimited: The Silver Age – Broken Empire]*

1967 – The second Peregrine battles and defeats the Warlike Manchu, who is in possession of the Mayan Tablet that Doctor Satan coveted in '43. Evelyn Davies dies. *["The Four Peregrines," The Peregrine Volume Two]*

1970 – William Davies (the second Peregrine) commits suicide by jumping from a Manhattan rooftop. Emma Davies (Max's daughter and William's sister) becomes the Peregrine one week later, in February. *["The Four Peregrines," The Peregrine Volume Two]*

1973 – The third Peregrine is accompanied by Kayla Kaslov (daughter of Leonid Kaslov) on a trip to Brazil, where the two women defeat the Black Annis and claim the Mayan Tablet that's popped up over the course of three decades. Emma gives it to her father, who in turn passes it on to Catalyst (Nathaniel Caine) *["The Four Peregrines," The Peregrine Volume Two]*

~1985 – Max resumes operating as the Peregrine, adventuring sporadically. Due to various magical events, he remains far more active than most men his age. The reasons for Emma giving up the role are unknown at this time.

Events depicted in the years 2006 forward occur in one of many possible futures for The Peregrine. As revealed in Volume Two of The Peregrine Chronicles, the events of 2006 onward may — or may not — be the ultimate future of Max Davies.

2006 – The Black Mass Barrier rises, enveloping the world in a magical field. The World of Shadows merges with Earth. Fiona Grace (descended from Eobard) becomes a worldwide celebrity, partially due to her failure to stop the Black Mass Barrier. *["Black Mass," The Peregrine Volume One]*

2009 – Ian Morris meets Max Davies and becomes the new Peregrine. He meets Fiona Grace. Max dies at some point immediately following this. *["Black Mass," The Peregrine Volume One]*

2010 – The Ian Morris Peregrine and Fiona Grace deal with the threat of Baron Samedi *["The Curse of Baron Samedi," The Peregrine Volume Three]*. Ian Morris briefly battles a confused Gideon Black in New York [The Second Book of Babylon]

2011 – Gideon Black, Daniel Higgins, Jennifer Black, Topaz and Johnny Galahad become embroiled in a series of strange events in London. Jennifer temporarily becomes the host for the Spirit of Retribution and engages in a deadly war of wills with Damien, the son of Lucifer. In the end, Daniel is restored to life and resumes his role as Babylon's host. *[The Second Book of Babylon]*

2012 – The fourth Peregrine (Ian Morris) receives the Mayan Tablet from Catalyst, who tells him that the world will end on December 21, 2012 unless something is done. Using the tablet, Ian attempts to take control of the magic spell that will end the world. Aided by the spirits of the three previous Peregrines, he succeeds, though it costs him his life. He is survived by his lover (Fiona Grace) and their unborn child. Max Davies is reborn as a man in his late twenties and becomes the Peregrine again. *["The Four Peregrines," The Peregrine Volume Two]*

2014 – The Black Mass Barrier falls and magic slowly begins to recede back to its pre-2006 levels.

2019 – Lilith journeys to Atlanta where she teams with The Peregrine and Pam Shields to combat The Caretaker. *[The Chronicles of Lilith]*

ABOUT THE AUTHOR

Barry Reese has carved out a reputation as one of the leading members of the New Pulp Movement. He's written for Marvel Comics, Moonstone Books, Pro Se Press, Airship 27 and more. He's best known for his shared universe of pulp adventurers - it includes **THE PEREGRINE**, **GRAVEDIGGER** and **LAZARUS GRAY**. He is an English teacher by day.

If you're interested in finding out more about his prolific writing career, check out **http://www.barryreese.net/**

Made in the USA
Las Vegas, NV
26 May 2022

49398164R00103